To All My Fans, With Love, From Sylvie

To All My Fans, With Love, From Sylvie

Ellen Conford

LIZZIE
SKURNICK
BOOKS

Brooklyn, New York

Printed in the United States
Reissue Edition
10 9 8 7 6 5 4 3 2 1

Please direct inquiries to:
Lizzie Skurnick Books
an imprint of Ig Publishing
392 Clinton Avenue #1S
Brooklyn, NY 11238
www.igpub.com

Library of Congress Cataloging-in-Publication Data

Conford, Ellen.
  To all my fans, with love, from Sylvie / Ellen Conford.
      pages cm
  Originally published by Little, Brown, 1982.
  Summary: Afraid of her foster father's advances, fifteen-year-old
Sylvia flees and is aided by Walter and Vic who have different mo-
tives for helping her.
  ISBN 978-1-939601-01-8 (pbk.)
  [1. Sexual harassment--Fiction. 2. Runaways--Fiction.] I. Title.
  PZ7.C7593To 2013
  [Fic]--dc23

To Dennis Bernstein,
Fran Chernowsky,
and Susan Pfeffer,
whom I'd love even
if I didn't have to

Chapter 1

June 10, 1956

Dear Mom,

    Even though you will probably never get this, like you never got any of the other letters I wrote you because I never mailed them, I am writing anyway to tell you I am finally going to "take the plunge" and set out for Hollywood.

    As you know—well, I guess you don't know, but you would if you had gotten my letters—people have always told me I ought to be in the movies because I am so pretty. I am not bragging or anything, I am just saying what people tell me. Anyway, I can't stay here anymore because of certain reasons which I cannot go into, but they are the same reasons why I had trouble in the two other places and I don't see that it is going to get any better even if they move me again.

    I made a very careful plan about how I am going to get to California, so don't think I am just rushing into this without knowing what I'm doing. I am fifteen now and when I'm all dressed up I look at least eighteen or nineteen and I can take care of myself.

    Well, when you go to the movies, or if they have movies where you are, look for me on the silver screen. Only don't look for the name Sylvie Krail, because I am changing it. I have not definitely decided on my stage name yet but I hope you will recognize my face, even though you haven't seen me since I was

I crumpled up the letter and threw my pen down on the desk. I don't know why I bother writing to my mother. I don't even have her address. All I know is that she's locked up someplace in a home for drunk people and has been there since I was three years old. At least, that's what everyone always told me. Not in those exact words, but I figured it out.

But sometimes I need somebody to talk to and there isn't anybody, so I write to my mother, and while I'm writing I can pretend she's really listening and will write back and give me advice about the problems I'm having.

I pulled out the bottom drawer of my desk and reached all the way back in to make sure the envelope was still there. My fingers touched it, I could feel the bulge of it, nice and fat because it was stuffed with mostly small bills. $137. It took me almost three years to save that money.

"Sylvie!"

I slammed the drawer shut just in time. Uncle Ted walked into my room without knocking, like he always does. It took me a while, but I learned that the only safe place to undress was in the bathroom with the door locked. Even in my own room on the hottest days I can't just sit around in shortie pajamas like other people do. So even though it was June, I had my flannel bathrobe wrapped around me, tied good and tight.

"Are you sure you won't come to church with us, Sylvie?" Uncle Ted stood over me, looking even taller than six feet, because I was sitting down and had to crane my neck to look up at him.

"I can't today," I said, making my voice sound weak and sick. "I'm really not feeling very well."

"Poor Sylvie." Uncle Ted put his hand on my forehead like he was feeling if I had a fever. He moved his hand down the side of my face to my neck. My whole body clenched up.

"Maybe I'd better stay home with you," he said softly. "In case you need something."

"No!" I said too loudly. "I mean, you have to drive Aunt Grace and the twins to church. How will they get there if you don't go?"

His gray eyes seemed to look right through me. He dropped his hand to his side.

"What are you writing?" he asked suddenly, his voice now all hearty and cheerful. He reached for the crumpled paper on my desk. I grabbed it and stuck it in my pocket.

"A fan letter. To James Dean."

"James Dean is dead," Uncle Ted said, frowning. "He's been dead for almost a year."

"But he still gets more fan mail than any other star in Hollywood."

"That doesn't make any sense. Why are you writing a letter to a dead person?"

Why was I writing a letter to my mother? Writing to a dead actor made just as much sense.

"Because he's my favorite star," I said.

"But—"

"Ted!" Aunt Grace's voice was sharp under my window. "We'll be late for church."

Uncle Ted walked over to the window and waved. "Be right down, hon. Just checking on Sylvie."

"You better go," I said. I put my hand against my stomach as if it hurt. "I'm just going to lie down and rest."

"I hope you feel better. Remember, Uncle Ted's famous barbecued hamburgers when we get back."

I made a face, like the thought of eating made me sick. "Gee, I don't know. . .

"Here, come on, I'll tuck you into bed." Uncle Ted took my arm and pushed me toward the bed.

"I can get into bed myself," I said. "I'm not a baby anymore."

"You certainly aren't," he muttered.

"TED!"

I dived into bed and pulled the sheet up to my chin.

"Coming, Grace!" he yelled. He leaned over me. "A little good-bye kiss for Uncle Ted?" he asked teasingly.

I turned my head away. "I might be catching," I said, and then groaned like I was in pain.

He brushed my ear with his lips and patted my hip. "See you later."

I pulled my knees up to my chest and mumbled good-bye into the pillow. I didn't relax until I heard the front door slam. Even though I was nearly sweating to death under the covers in my flannel bathrobe, I didn't move a muscle until I heard the Chevrolet pull out of the driveway, brake, and squeal off down the block.

I breathed out with a whoosh. I felt like I'd been holding my breath for the last five minutes. And even if I hadn't actually been holding it in my chest, I was holding it in my head.

I threw the covers off, jumped out of bed, and untied the cord of the bathrobe. I was dripping with sweat. I wiped my face and neck on one sleeve, then threw the robe on the floor and kicked it under the bed. Hollywood is warm and sunny. I'd never need flannel bathrobes there. Not to keep out the cold, and not to protect me from "uncles" either.

Uncle Ted and Aunt Grace aren't my real aunt and uncle, of course. They just told me to call them that because Mr. and Mrs. Tyson sounded too formal, when I was going to be part of their family, just like their daughter.

I figured I had about an hour and a half before they came back from church. I wished I could take a nice, cool shower, but there wasn't time. Everything had to be packed and my hatbox and suitcase had to be hidden before they got back from church.

Church. That was a laugh. Uncle Ted going to church and singing the hymns and praying to God and looking all Christian and holy five minutes after trying to tuck me into bed. What if they knew what he was really like? What if Aunt Grace knew? I bet she'd drop dead right in the middle of her paint-by-numbers oil picture of the Last Supper.

But maybe she wouldn't. Maybe she'd look straight at me and say, "Sylvie, you must be imagining things." That's what had happened the first time, when I was twelve.

"It's a misunderstanding," Mr. Framer had told the social worker, holding his hands spread out wide as if to show her he had nothing to hide. "It must be some sort of misunderstanding."

"The child has such a vivid imagination," Mrs. Framer said. "You know how she's always playacting, doing impersonations. And of course, she's not used to the natural affection of a father for a daughter. That's why she's here, after all."

Even though I was only twelve, I knew I wasn't imagining things. Maybe I wasn't used to the natural affection of a father for a daughter, but I knew darned well that wasn't what Mr. Framer wanted. I was mature for my age. That's really why all the trouble started. That's why I had to get out. Right then. Before it was too late.

One thing I learned from the Framers was that no one was going to take my word over the word of a perfectly respectable-looking foster father. They didn't believe me that time, and they would never believe me.

Everyone agreed that even if I'd been making up the story about Mr. Framer trying to get his hands on me, it was probably the best thing all around for me to be placed with another family.

Which is what happened. Which is how I got to the O'Connors'. Which is where the whole thing started all over again.

"Come see what I've got, Sylvie. Come see what old Dad has for you."

"What?" I'd ask suspiciously.

It would never turn out to be anything that great, but for some reason, whatever it was he wanted to show me, I'd have to sit on his lap to see it.

It didn't take me a long time to catch on.

I spent a whole year making sure I was never alone in the house with Mr. O'Connor, never alone in the same room with him, unless Mrs. O'Connor was nearby, and never, *never* getting undressed unless I was in the bathroom with the door locked. Mr. O'Connor had walked into my room without knocking at least three different times while I was getting ready for bed. A decent person would have said, "Oh, excuse me, I should have knocked," and gone right out and shut the door behind him.

Not Mr. O'Connor. All three times he just stood there, staring, licking his lips, while I grabbed for something to cover myself with. And then he'd say something like, "My, my, aren't you getting to be a big girl?"

He was horrible. He was disgusting. And *old*. He must have been at least forty-five, though I'm not very good at figuring out ages. He had a big beer belly and no hair on the front of his chest and he chewed with his mouth open and talked at the same time.

There were two other foster children there too. Brothers. Georgie and Ernie. They were younger than I was, and I think Mrs. O'Connor took me to be a built-in baby-sitter for them. But they were no trouble. They were kind of quiet and watched television a lot, and since the O'Connors didn't go out very much, there wasn't a lot of baby-sitting to do.

Not for the O'Connors, anyway. But I found there were other people who needed baby-sitters, and I started right in three weeks after I saw how it was going to be with Mr. O'Connor. I sat for people almost every Friday and Saturday night, unless I had to stay with Georgie and Ernie, and I saved everything I could in a red-plaid rayon change purse that I kept pinned to my pajamas when I was asleep and inside my underpants when I went out.

What else could I do? If I went and told the social worker that Mr. O'Connor was exactly the same as Mr. Framer, would she believe me? She didn't believe me before, and if I told the same story again she'd probably be convinced I was a troublemaking liar.

I pulled the suitcase down from the top shelf of my closet. It was the color of straw, with brown bands and a brown handle, and even with nothing in it, it was heavy. A neighbor had packed it with my things after my grandmother died and the social worker came to take me to the Framers'.

I was only seven, and too little to carry it myself. The social worker took the suitcase in one hand and held me with the other as we went out to her car. I took the suitcase with me when I left the Framers' for the O'Connors'. That time, the social worker didn't carry it for me. She didn't hold my hand, either.

Now I knew I had to take only the most absolutely necessary things with me, but since I didn't have that many clothes anyway, it wasn't a big deal deciding what to pack. I was going to take only the clothes that made me look eighteen, and my cosmetics, of course, but they would go in my hatbox.

That hatbox was one of the very few things I'd bought for myself out of my savings. It was beautiful, ivory-colored simulated leather, and even though it cost $14.99 on sale, I knew I had to have it. I'm very realistic and practical, and I knew it might take me a while after I got to Hollywood to get my first break in the movies, so I figured I would do some modeling until I was discovered. A lot of movie stars start that way, and models make sometimes $35 to $50 *an hour.* And all the models go from job to job with their stuff in a hatbox, just like mine. It's a model's *trademark,* her hatbox, and if I had one, they'd know I was a professional just by looking at me.

The only things I regretted leaving behind were my movie magazines. I'd read them already, of course, and they were all cut up where I had clipped out pictures of my favorite stars, but I still liked to go back and look at them and read the articles about how the stars live.

They're very helpful, some of those articles. I've learned everything I know about how to be a star from movie magazines. That's why I look so much older than fifteen, and why I'm more sophisticated than other girls my age. Every month at least one of the magazines has an article on "Makeup Tips from the Stars," and I practically *study* those articles.

So I looked at the pile of magazines on the floor of my closet and sighed. First, I thought I might just take the ones with stories about James Dean and Natalie Wood. She's my ideal. We have practically *identical* eyebrows. The first thing I'm going to buy when I get my break in the movies is a gold slave bracelet, like she has. She's always photographed with that slave bracelet on. It's sort of her trademark.

We're a lot alike in other ways, besides just having the same eyebrows. She's only a couple of years older than me, but she's also very mature for her age, and very sophisticated. She says her biggest problem is that she smokes too much. I don't smoke yet, but I guess I'm going to have to start pretty soon.

Anyway, I started going through the pile of magazines, and realized that almost every one of them had a story on James Dean and a lot of them had articles on Natalie Wood. That's why I'd bought them in the first place. So I gave up on the idea of taking any of them, and just put my scrapbook on the bottom of the suitcase.

All the best pictures were in there anyway. Lots of James Dean, all the ones of Natalie, plus Tab Hunter, Rock Hudson, Elvis, William Holden, etc. Besides, I told myself, once I started being in the movies I'd have plenty of money to buy all the magazines I wanted. I'd probably even *be* in some of them!

I packed my underwear and shoes on top of the scrapbook. I didn't have any tissue paper, which was too bad, because in this article on "How to Pack for Traveling" by Joan Crawford, she said tissue paper is an absolute *must* for keeping things from wrinkling and for wrapping shoes in. I only had two pairs of shoes that I was going to pack and one that I was going to wear, so I went downstairs to the kitchen and got some wax paper to wrap them in.

I unplugged Aunt Grace's white plastic radio that she keeps on the kitchen counter and took it upstairs with me so I could have some music while I worked. Another thing I wanted more than anything in the world was my own portable radio, but I just couldn't afford to spend $19.95 on a luxury like that. When I was famous I would have a radio in every room. The *Photoplay* story about me would explain, "So she can have music wherever she goes." Maybe that could be my trademark.

I plugged the radio in next to my bed and finished packing my suitcase.

Elvis was singing "Blue Suede Shoes" when I started packing the hatbox. I sort of bounced around the room, picking up my stuff, opening drawers, singing the words along with him. I knew them by heart, of course.

I had to take all my cosmetics and makeup with me. Those were the only other things besides magazines that I spent money on, but I knew they were worth it. The right makeup can transform a merely pretty girl into a true beauty, and there are lots of merely pretty girls who think they can get into the movies. I would be competing with them for my big break, and like I said, I'm realistic enough to know I have to be as beautiful as possible to make it in Hollywood.

But I also planned to live out of that hatbox on my trip to California, so I had to get some underwear and a pair of shortie pajamas and a change of clothes in there too. I couldn't keep opening and closing the big suitcase every time I needed something. With all those bottles and jars and compacts and things, I was a little worried about stuff breaking, but I wrapped some of the breakables in my thick white crew socks and hoped for the best.

I glanced at the clock on my night table. It was noon already! Aunt Grace and Uncle Ted would be back in fifteen minutes. I looked around the little room trying to see if I had forgotten anything.

I pulled the desk chair over to the closet and hauled the big suitcase up to the top shelf. I nearly broke my arms trying to wedge it back on the shelf where it belonged, but I got it. I pushed the chair back under the desk and stuck the hatbox all the way over to one side of the closet behind my crinolines, where you couldn't see it when you opened the door.

The crinolines were another problem, but I had solved that very cleverly, I thought. I absolutely had to take them with me, because I needed them to wear under my best dress, which was a pink Teena Paige with a square neck and a beautiful full skirt. Naturally I had to take that, for interviews and dates and things, and naturally I couldn't wear it without three crinolines underneath it so the skirt would stand out right.

So I decided to wear it on my trip, then I wouldn't have to worry about fitting the crinolines in my suitcase because I'd be wearing them under the dress.

I had everything figured out perfectly.

I heard the sound of the Chevrolet in the driveway. Four doors slammed and one of the twins yelled, "Sylvie, Sylvie, we're home!"

So soon! I snapped the radio off and jumped into bed. I pulled the covers over me.

They were ten minutes early. It's a good thing I hadn't stopped to take a shower.

"Sylvie?" It was Uncle Ted. I could hear his footsteps coming up the stairs.

"Sylvie, how are you feeling? It's barbecue time!"

With no one in the house, I'd forgotten to shut the door. I turned toward the wall and pretended to be asleep.

Chapter 2

"Sylvie! Sylvie! Daddy's going to barbecue!"

Honey and Bunny, the twins, came barreling into the room right behind Uncle Ted. One of them jumped on my bed. I turned over slowly, pretending I was just waking up.

"Get off the bed, Honey," Uncle Ted said irritably. "You might catch what Sylvie's got."

"What've you got, Sylvie?" Honey bounced on my bed until Uncle Ted grabbed her under the arms and lifted her off.

"A stomachache," I said. "I wish you wouldn't bounce on my bed. It makes me feel sicker."

"I'm not bouncing anymore," Honey said. But she was. She was bouncing on the floor, she and Bunny, jiggling around in their matching yellow sunback dresses, like jumping jacks that had to go to the bathroom.

"Now you two get out of here," Uncle Ted said sternly. "Sylvie isn't feeling well and you're just making her feel worse."

Hardy har har, I thought. Just like he was really concerned. There was only one reason he wanted them out of my room and it had nothing to do with my pretend sickness.

"That's okay," I said. I made my voice sound brave and noble, like I was really suffering but determined not to show it. Like Judy Garland in *A Star Is Born* when she gets the Academy Award. "They don't bother me."

"You can't even *eat*, Sylvie?" Bunny said. "Not even hamburgers and hot dogs?"

"I don't think so. Oohh," I groaned, and held my stomach. It was absolutely vital that they think I was too sick to go to school tomorrow, which was one of the two reasons I had to start being sick today. The other was so that I could get out of going to church with them and get my packing done.

"Not even *barbecue* hamburgers?" Honey said, like she could hardly believe it.

I could have kicked myself for saying I had a stomachache instead of a headache or sore throat or something, because I really was hungry. I should have sneaked something to eat while they were at church. I hadn't eaten anything since supper last night and I was starving. And now it looked like I wouldn't get to eat until tomorrow.

Aunt Grace came into the room. "How are you feeling, Sylvie? Any better?" She pulled off her white gloves and fanned herself with them. "My, it certainly is hot up here. You must be perishing." She took off her little white hat and patted her Blonde Mink curls. (Courtesy of Mr. Anthony's Salon de Beauté.)

"Sylvie is sick," Honey said. "In her stomach."

"Sylvie might throw up," Bunny added. She sounded like she was almost excited at that idea.

"Now shoo, you two, and change out of your dresses and leave Sylvie alone. Goodness, Sylvie, I wish you had come to church with us. It just isn't the easiest thing in the world to pray and keep your eye on those two at the same time. They were just impossible without you."

I'll bet they were. I noticed it never occurred to Aunt

Grace to worry about how *I* was supposed to pray and keep the twins from leaping all over the church like they were in a Martin and Lewis movie.

"We prayed for the President," Honey said importantly. "That he should get better."

"That he shouldn't die," Bunny said, nodding.

"And we prayed that Elvis Presley *should* die," Honey said.

"Oh, Honey, you're all mixed up," Aunt Grace laughed. "That was the sermon. You should have been there, Sylvie. The sermon was very appropriate. It was all about this rock-and-roll music."

"Did he really say Elvis should die?" I asked, horrified. Dr. Cannon could get pretty worked up about juvenile delinquency and communism and all, but I never heard him actually wish for somebody to die.

"No, he just said the *music* ought to die out and probably would. He certainly doesn't think much of that Elvis, though, I'll tell you that."

Boy, was I sorry I missed that sermon! It was probably the first time in history Dr. Cannon preached something I was interested in.

"All right, look," Uncle Ted said impatiently. "Are we going to get this barbecue started or what? Sylvie, you want to come down and lie on the patio where it's cooler? Even if you don't want to eat—"

"No, maybe later. I just want to rest. I feel real weak and dizzy."

"All right. Maybe you can have some tea and toast later," Aunt Grace said. "Now, come on everybody, and let Sylvie rest in peace."

Finally! They all cleared out of my room, including Uncle Ted. I heard the sounds of drawers and closets opening and closing as they changed from their Sunday clothes into their backyard clothes.

Soon the twins were shrieking in the backyard at the fire, and the smell of charcoal smoke began to drift up through my window. I got out of bed and went into the bathroom. I washed all over with a washcloth and cold water then patted myself dry with a towel and dusted with Cashmere Bouquet talcum powder. I didn't have to worry about Uncle Ted coming upstairs as long as the barbecue was going.

He loved to barbecue. He made a real big deal out of it, like he was chef for the day and no one else could turn a hamburger on the grill like he could.

Aunt Grace acted the same way, and it was such a joke! She got him this barbecue apron with a picture of a chef in a tall white hat holding a big platter of hamburgers and saying, "Come and get it!" And the only thing he actually did was to light the charcoal and turn over the hamburgers and hot dogs. Because Aunt Grace mixed up the hamburger and squeezed it into flat patties, and made the potato salad and the coleslaw, unless she bought them from the delicatessen. And I peeled the cellophane off each hot dog, so what was the big deal about Uncle Ted doing all the cooking?

But everybody had to make a fuss about how good his hamburgers were, and you couldn't get that charcoal taste in a restaurant, and even a hot dog at a baseball game didn't taste this good, all black and puffy and squirting juice out when you bit into it.

What it was, really, was that when we had barbecues, Aunt Grace and Uncle Ted could act like we were all one big, happy, normal American family, just like in the article in *Look* magazine, with pictures showing how the weekend barbecue is the most popular way for families to practice togetherness.

We would come home from church, where everyone knew how good and kind Uncle Ted and Aunt Grace were to poor Sylvie, taking her in even though they had two children of their own to care for. I guess no one ever stopped to think that that might be just the reason Aunt Grace and Uncle Ted took me in. Maybe the O'Connors hadn't needed a baby-sitter that much, but here I was practically the twins' second mother. And then there was the money the county paid them every month. That didn't hurt either.

Anyway, when the church service was over, Uncle Ted was all cheerful and smiling, seeing all those men he sold insurance to, slapping people on the back and praising Dr. Cannon's "thought-provoking" sermon and probably feeling so all-around noble and fatherly and religious that he completely forgot all the times he came into my room to "kiss me good-night."

And Aunt Grace would be showing off the twins in their matching dresses, and putting her arm around me to show everyone I was just like her own daughter, and telling Dr. Cannon that his sermon was so inspiring, it really gave her something to *think* about. And a minute later she'd ask Uncle Ted whether she should try to make a heart-shaped marshmallow Jell-O mold for her canasta group the next day, or would it get all mushed up when she tried to un-mold it?

So, feeling all warm and churchy, they'd go home and change and set us all up in the backyard, just like we were posing for those pictures in *Look* magazine. The perfect family, doing what the perfect family does every weekend. They probably wished a photographer would come and take a picture of us and print it in some magazine so everyone could see what a perfect family we were.

But I bet Uncle Ted wouldn't want any photographers around at night. Say, ten o'clock at night. Upstairs. In my room.

I turned the radio back on. Harry Belafonte was singing "Sylvie."

It was like a sign. I love that song. It's just like it was written for me. Except some of the boys in school sing it to me and change the words, so they sing it: "Sylvie, Sylvie, I'm so hot and dry. Sylvie, Sylvie, can't you hear, can't you hear me callin', Bring me little mm mm Sylvie, Bring me little mm mm now-ow . . ." Instead of "water," they sing "mm mm" in a really dirty way.

I try to ignore it and to just walk away with my head high to show them how juvenile I think they are. And they really are. They're just juvenile babies. None of the boys in school are mature enough for me and it makes them mad because I won't even look at them, so that's how they get back at me.

A lot of them try to act like James Dean and dress like him and let their cigarettes hang off their lips till you think they're going to set fire to themselves. But it takes a lot more than a pair of jeans and a garrison belt to be James Dean. They just end up looking hoody, and some of them really are JDs, but the thing is, you know James Dean *isn't*; you know that he's just misunderstood, and on the inside he's good and it just takes the right person to understand him and sympathize with him for the goodness to come out.

These guys who imitate him, they don't know how he suffers, they don't understand how he really hurts inside. So they'll never be James Dean because they don't know what it feels like to *hurt* so much that you can hardly talk to people.

Anyway, another interesting thing about that song, "Sylvie," besides that it's my name is that it's the first song I ever heard with the word "damn" in it. I didn't know you could say that on the radio, but it's in the song, and they play it on the radio. And none of the rock-and-roll songs I like have any swear words in them, so I don't understand why people are more upset by rock and roll than by "Sylvie."

Also, I think Harry Belafonte is beautiful. Not just handsome, but beautiful, and I never thought any man was beautiful before. He isn't in too many magazines so I only have one picture of him, but I love to look at it and imagine him kissing me. Even if he is a Negro, I don't care, it doesn't make him any less beautiful, and when I hear him sing "Sylvie," I imagine him holding me in his arms and singing the words softly right into my ear.

The barbecue smells really began to get to me, so I got into a pair of capri pants and my striped boat-neck top and went downstairs.

Uncle Ted was toasting marshmallows on the grill. "Well, well, how's the patient?"

"Sylvie, Sylvie!" the twins screamed, like they hadn't seen me for a year. "Marshmallows! Daddy's toasting marshmallows!"

"Yes, I see."

"Are you feeling better?" Aunt Grace asked.

"Not really. It's just so hot up in my room."

"Sit down on the chaise longue," she said. "It's nice and cool down here now. Would you like to try some toast and tea?"

"Well," I said doubtfully, "at least I could try." I really would have liked a hot dog, but a person with a sick stomach couldn't ask for a hot dog. It was toast, or starve to death.

"I'll make it," I said, as Aunt Grace started to get up from the redwood table.

I went through the back door into the kitchen and made the tea and toast. I ate it there, where nobody could see me wolfing it down. I had four pieces of toast with chunks of Velveeta on them and two cups of tea.

I went back outside, holding my stomach.

"I don't know if eating was such a good idea, Aunt Grace."

"Oh, dear. Maybe we'd better call Dr. Fitch if you're still feeling this way tomorrow." I could see Aunt Grace didn't like that idea too much. Monday was canasta day. Well, I didn't want the doctor either. I had to be just sick enough to stay home from school, but not sick enough to have Aunt Grace miss her game at Millie Reemer's.

"Are you going to throw up, Sylvie? Are you going to throw up?"

"Stop it, Honey!" Aunt Grace said sharply.

"I better go back to bed."

"Take the little fan from our room, Sylvie," Uncle Ted called after me as I went inside. "That'll stir the air around, anyway."

"Okay. Thanks."

The afternoon dragged on forever. I lay on my bed with some of my magazines, the fan whirring away on my desk, the radio playing the top twenty-five songs of the week.

I began counting how many hours I had left to live in this house. Each hour that dragged by seemed longer than the year I had already been here.

I don't really know for sure why Aunt Grace and Uncle Ted took me in, especially because the way I got myself out of the O'Connors' was by being as much trouble as possible without actually being a JD.

Like I said, I knew the social worker wouldn't believe me if I told the truth about Mr. O'Connor and what he was trying to do, so the only thing I could think of was to make the O'Connors want to get rid of me.

I started not answering them when they talked to me. I didn't do anything they told me to. I went out of the house and wouldn't come back till all hours of the night. If I didn't have a baby-sitting job I'd usually go to the movies and then just walk around till I was sure it was late enough for them to be plenty worried about me.

I knew what I was doing was making Ernie and Georgie very nervous and upset, but I couldn't help it. I had to get out of there. I was a nervous wreck myself, from having spent all those months practically running from Mr. O'Connor, and not always getting away. Somehow he always managed, no matter how cagey I thought I was being, to get his hands on me one way or another, a couple of times a week.

When I started acting like a real "troubled teenager," Mr. O'Connor got madder and madder.

One night when I came in late from baby-sitting, Mr. O'Connor was dozing in front of the television. All the lights in the house were off. I closed the door real softly behind me, but just then the TV blared out the "Star-Spangled Banner" and Mr. O'Connor woke up and saw me.

"This is a fine hour for you to come waltzing in," he said, snapping on the floor lamp next to his chair.

"How do you know what time it is?" I said. "You were asleep."

"Don't be fresh with me, young lady, or I'll teach you some manners with this." He held up his fist.

"You lay a hand on me," I said, my voice all shaky, "and I'll tell the social worker and you'll never get any other kids at eighty bucks a month."

He dropped his fist to his side. I guess the thought of losing the money the county paid for the three of us made him think twice about hitting me.

Then he got this real sly look on his face.

"Why do you have to be that way, Sylvie?" he said. "Why do you always have to make me mad? I don't want to be mad at you. I don't want to hit you. I want us to be friends."

He started walking toward me, a phony-kind smile on his face.

I darted toward the hall to run to my room, but for a heavy guy he was pretty fast. He grabbed my arm and pulled me against him.

"Sylvie, be nice. I'll be nice to you, you'll see how nice I can be." He slobbered on my neck, his fingers pawing at my collar.

My heart hammered in my chest. I was smothering, I was suffocating, my face pressed into his shirtfront, his sweaty hands grabbing at my buttons.

I socked him in the ribs and screamed.

"You dirty old pig! You fat old pig! Don't you dare touch me!"

I ran down the hall to my room, just as Mrs. O'Connor came running to see what the noise was about.

"Sylvie, what is it? What's going on?"

"Ask *him!*" I yelled. "Ask the fat old *pig* yourself."

"Sylvie!"

I slammed my door shut and threw myself across the bed, crying like crazy.

I was scared to death. I was crying because I was mad, but I was crying because I was really terrified, too. I'd made him *too* angry. It wasn't my fault, this time I hadn't started it, but I'd made him so mad I knew he was going to get me. He was big and he was strong and he was an adult, and he'd figure out a way to lie to the social worker so she'd believe him and not me.

It wasn't going to be all fake fatherly smiles and accidental touching anymore. He wasn't going to bother to pretend after this. It was too late for pretending. I had hit him. He knew he wasn't fooling me. And he was going to get me. He was going to *force* me.

Even crying into my pillow, gasping for breath, I could hear him yelling. "Impossible! Incorrigible! . . . don't know what gets into her." I couldn't hear what Mrs. O'Connor was saying, she was talking too softly, but I was sure she would believe whatever lies he was telling her.

And then she'd go back to bed and he'd stay up and wait, until he was sure she was asleep, until he thought I was asleep. . . .

I groaned and slammed my fist into my pillow. *No!*

I hauled myself off the bed and looked around the room. There was a big, old oak chest of drawers next to the door. I ran to it, leaned my shoulder against it, and pushed. I couldn't budge it.

Still crying, still hardly able to catch my breath, I opened all four drawers and dumped the things in them on the floor. Then I pulled the drawers out and pushed the dresser against the door. I put the drawers back in and threw all the stuff back into the drawers.

"Sylvie, what are you doing? Sylvie, what are you moving around in there?"

I fell back on the bed, exhausted. The doorknob turned, rattled, the door thunked against the dresser but didn't move another inch.

"Open the door, Sylvie! Open the door this instant!"

I didn't answer.

I never spoke another word to Mr. or Mrs. O'Connor.

I sat straight up in bed all night, staring at the dresser.

The next afternoon, Miss Jenks, the social worker, came to take me to "Aunt Grace" and "Uncle Ted" Tyson.

So like I say, I don't know why Aunt Grace and Uncle Ted took me in, what with the reputation I had from the Framers and the O'Connors. Especially since I was the first foster child they'd ever had. And why they'd want to trust someone like me—or the kind of person they must have thought I was—with their six-year-old twin daughters was another thing I couldn't figure. Aunt Grace talked a lot about "Christian charity," so the only thing I could think was, maybe taking me was a way of making Brownie points with God.

Anyhow, after a couple of weeks they told Miss Jenks they couldn't believe I was the same girl she'd told them about.

Well, I wasn't. I hadn't been the girl she'd told them about in the first place. That had been an act. I really am a very good actress, which is why I know I can get in the movies. It takes more than just a pretty face. More than just a beautiful face, even. It takes talent, which I proved I have.

"Sylvie, Ed Sullivan is on! Sylvie, come on and watch Ed Sullivan with us! Maybe Señor Wences'll be on!" Honey and Bunny both came rushing into my room.

"Is it that late?" I felt sort of groggy. Somehow the afternoon had passed after I stopped counting hours. I had missed supper. I must have fallen asleep.

"Sylvie, come *on!*" Bunny said. "You'll miss the famous people in the studio audience. Maybe James Dean'll be there."

"James Dean is dead, Bunny. He can't be in the studio audience."

"Maybe President Eisenhower then."

"He's in the hospital. Remember? You prayed for him."

"Maybe the prayers worked. Come on, Sylvie, you have to watch with us. You always watch with us."

"Okay, okay."

They each took one of my hands and practically pulled me out of bed. I looked at them in their seersucker nightgowns, their blond curls frizzy from the heat and their bath.

I hugged them against my hips. Next week, when I wasn't here, would they miss me? Would they wonder where I was?

Maybe some Sunday night they'd be watching Ed Sullivan and the camera would pick out a famous face in the audience and Ed would say, "And over here we have that up-and-coming new star—" and Honey and Bunny would start screaming, "It's Sylvie, it's Sylvie!"

Only, by then I wouldn't be Sylvie anymore.

After eleven o'clock tomorrow morning, I'd never be Sylvie Krail again.

Chapter 3

"Sylvie, I really don't like to go off and leave you alone like this."

"Oh, Aunt Grace, you've left me alone before."

"But not when you're sick. It's different."

"You can leave me Mrs. Reemer's number and I can call you if I need anything. I don't want you to miss your canasta game on account of me." I used my sick-but-brave voice again. She *had* to go to that canasta game.

"Well, that's true. I'm only ten minutes away, after all."

"I'm a big girl, Aunt Grace. You know I can take care of myself."

"I guess you can. And if you're still feeling bad when I come home, we can call the doctor then."

"Sure, that's right. You go and have a good time. I know how you look forward to your canasta."

The doorbell rang.

"Oh, there's Betty already." Aunt Grace patted her hair and tugged at her turquoise pedal pushers. She ran to the twins' room and called out the window. "I'll be right there!"

She came back into my room. "I'll see you later, dear. I hope you feel better. You just rest and take care of yourself."

The doorbell rang again.

"I *must* run." She fluttered her fingers at me and hurried out of my room.

"Good-bye, Aunt Grace," I said softly.

I waited until I heard Betty Kramer's car pulling away, and then I jumped out of bed. The first thing I did was to run downstairs and make myself a bologna sandwich, because I was starving from not having eaten anything but toast since yesterday. I could only finish half of it. I guess I was too nervous to eat. I filled up much faster than I thought I would.

I took a shower and sprinkled myself all over with Cashmere Bouquet. I wished I had time to shampoo my hair, but it would have taken too long to dry. Even though I don't have oily-type hair, I like to wash it twice a week to keep it looking its best, and I hadn't shampooed since Friday. But I had to settle for just brushing Minipoo through it. I figured it would be all right since I wasn't wearing it loose, but in a French twist, which makes me look at least eighteen.

I pulled the suitcase down from the top of the closet. I nearly dropped it on the floor, it was so heavy. I put on all the crinolines and my pink dress and clipped my white pop beads around my neck. I pulled out the bottom drawer of the desk and yanked the envelope from the back. I put it inside the zipper pocket of my straw pocketbook.

I took a long, careful time with my makeup. I put on pressed powder and some rouge and black mascara and curled my eyelashes so they'd look even longer and more dramatic. I dabbed some "Strike Me Pink" lipstick onto my brush (all the stars tell you a lipstick brush is an absolute *must*) and outlined my lips. I filled them in with the lipstick, then blotted them on a tissue.

I stood back and looked at myself in the mirror. I looked like I could be in the movies, I thought. And with my French twist and my gloves and my white slingback heels, I definitely looked eighteen. Maybe even twenty.

I lugged the suitcase and hatbox downstairs and put them next to the front door. In the kitchen Aunt Grace kept a pad that has "Shopping List" printed on it, with a little pencil attached.

I sat down at the table with the pad and wrote my good-bye note.

> *Dear Aunt Grace,*
>> *I'm going to my mother. I found out she is in a place in Rochester and I have to see her. I'm sorry to fool you like I did about being sick but it was the only way. Thank you for everything and don't worry about me. Say good-bye to the twins and Uncle Ted for me.*
>>> *Sincerely yours,*
>>> *Sylvie Krail*

I left the note on the table and went to call a taxi.

This was going to be the only tricky part of my plan. If Mrs. Bates next door saw me getting into the taxi with my suitcase, she'd know something was up. Betty Kramer was our neighbor on the other side, and she was with Aunt Grace at Millie Reemer's, and the neighbors across the street probably didn't know where Aunt Grace could be reached because she wasn't all that friendly with them.

But Mrs. Bates always did her laundry on Mondays, hanging it out on the turn-around clothes pole in the backyard, so I was hoping that's where she'd be when the taxi came.

The taxi company said the cab would be here in fifteen minutes. I told them I had to catch a train, and they said not to worry, the next train to the city wasn't for half an hour, so I sat down in the chair next to the front door to wait.

I thought that note was pretty smart. Like I told my mother in the letter, I had a very good plan of how to get away without being found and that note was part of my plan. Everybody would be looking for me all the way to Rochester, and I wasn't going in that direction at all. By the time they realized I wasn't in Rochester, I'd probably be in California. And they'd never think to look for me in California.

I couldn't sit still. Here I had planned this trip for months, years almost, and it was finally only ten minutes away from beginning, and I thought I'd die waiting for that last ten minutes to go by.

It wasn't so hot today, which I was glad about, because when it's very hot I sweat and my bangs get all limp and the angel wings on the side droop until they're flat. (Some people call them devil wings instead of angel wings, which I think is funny, that they should be called opposite things.) Anyway, they're like Brenda Starr in the comics wears her hair. They're not really bangs, they sort of swoop up and back on each side of my forehead. Some people have to set them to make them go that way, but my hair just waves there naturally.

I went to the kitchen to get some Kool-Aid and I thought, This is the last time I will ever see this kitchen. Part of me felt a little sad about leaving Aunt Grace and the twins, but I was too excited about my new life and my career to think about much else.

I was almost tempted to leave a separate note for Uncle

Ted, telling him the real reason why I was leaving, which he probably could guess anyway, but Aunt Grace might find it.

There was another reason I had to leave, but I could never tell that to anybody. Especially not to Uncle Ted.

A car honked twice outside. The taxi had come. I ran to the front door and threw it open. I hoped no one else would come to their front door at the sound of the horn.

I grabbed my pocketbook and my hatbox and pulled my suitcase out the door. I closed the door behind me and hurried down the walk to the cab.

I pushed the suitcase in the back before the driver could even offer to help me with it, and climbed in.

"The train station," I said.

"Okay." He shifted and the taxi squealed away from the curb. I looked back at the house, a little, salmon-colored box that was exactly the same as all the other houses on the block, except for the paint. I looked at the pink plastic flamingo on the front lawn. Nobody else on the block had a flamingo like that.

No one seemed to be watching out their windows, so I turned around and stared straight ahead as we turned the corner of Robin Lane. I fixed my eyes on the taxi driver's collar, and never once turned to look back.

Chapter 4

Dear Mom,

Well, here I am on my way to California! My plan worked out just as well as I expected. I think I was really clever about "covering my tracks." I'm not bragging or anything, but I've seen enough movies to know how to "lay a false trail" and that's what I did. For instance, I left a note saying I was going to visit you in Rochester, which I wish I was, but of course I don't know where you are, but I made them think I did. Then I had the taxi take me to the train station, but I didn't take the train to the city, like I told the driver I was going to. Instead I took a bus to the city and the subway to the Greyhound bus terminal and bought a ticket to

"My, I don't know how you can write on a moving bus like that."

I covered up my letter with my hand and turned to the woman next to me. She was pretty old, but she had a nice face.

"I can't even read on a moving vehicle," she said. "The letters start swimming around in front of my eyes, and first thing you know I've got one of my sick headaches."

We'd been riding for two hours. She must have been pretty bored, not being able to read and all. And with me sitting by the window, she didn't even have any scenery to look at.

I folded my letter and put it in my pocketbook.

"Oh, don't stop writing on my account," she said. "I didn't mean to bother you."

"That's okay. I was finished anyway. Would you like to sit by the window for a while?"

"Well, thank you, dear, that would be nice."

We switched places. "It's such a long trip," she said. "Maybe we could change every two hours."

"Okay."

She settled back in the seat and turned toward me. She hadn't even peeked out the window. I guess she wanted to talk. I didn't mind. I'd bought a movie magazine at the bus terminal, but I'd read the whole thing already.

I bought it because there was this big headline on the front cover: JAMES DEAN DID NOT DIE! I couldn't wait to read the article, so I sat right down on a bench in the waiting room and turned to the page where the story was, and of course it turned out that what they meant was James Dean's memory lives on in the hearts of his fans. I was pretty annoyed, but there were a lot of pictures with the article, so that was something.

Some of these magazines can be really sneaky. Like, for instance, I bought this magazine once because it had a story called "Why Tab Is Taboo to Me," by Natalie Wood. Well, of course I thought it would be all about why Natalie wouldn't get serious with Tab Hunter, even though all the magazines were running pictures of them on dates together, but what it turned out to be was that "Taboo" was Natalie's nickname for Tab. It wasn't so bad, though, even if it was sneaky, because there was a lot in it about Natalie and the kind of life she lives in Hollywood, and the actors she pals around with, like Nick Adams and Dennis Hopper and a lot of the younger up-and-coming stars.

I got to thinking how maybe, once I started working in movies, we would become friends, Natalie and me, because we were almost the same age and even if she is a little older, everyone in Hollywood would think I was eighteen, because that's what I was going to tell them. And I'd go around with her and have double dates and go to premieres together and meet all the teenage actors she knows.

Maybe even Tab Hunter. That would be okay with Natalie, because in the article it said she was only good friends with him. They are like brother and sister, so she wouldn't mind if I dated him, I'm sure.

I'm not all that hot to go with Tab Hunter, though. He's cute and all, but not one of my absolute top favorites. But I wouldn't turn him down if he asked me out.

But anyway, like I was saying, being a real expert on movie magazines, I know some of them can be very misleading. I keep buying them anyhow, but for the real truth about the stars you can only depend on *Photoplay* and *Modern Screen*. You know if you read it there you're getting the true facts.

"I'm going to Springfield, Ohio, to visit my son and grandchildren," the woman next to me said suddenly. "He's an assistant manager at the Sears, Roebuck store. I go twice a year to visit them."

"How many grandchildren do you have?" I didn't really care all that much, but I could see she wanted to talk.

"Well, John has twin boys—"

"Isn't that funny!" I said without thinking. "I have—" I stopped myself just in time. I'd been going to tell her about Honey and Bunny and that would have been a big goof. What if the police managed to track me down to the Greyhound bus station, even though I'd done such a good job of faking them out? If they started questioning people who had been on Greyhound buses, and this lady told them about sitting next to a girl who talked about twins named Honey and Bunny, they'd be hot on my trail.

"You have what? What were you going to say?"

"Nothing. I was just wondering if we were ever going to stop anyplace. I'm kind of hungry."

She nodded. "I think we're stopping in about an hour. You'll be able to freshen up and get something to eat then. How far are you traveling?"

Since she was getting off in Ohio, she wouldn't know I was going to Los Angeles unless I told her. Just in case, I thought I'd better not give her my real destination. But besides Los Angeles, I couldn't think where the bus might stop after Springfield. I'm not very good at geography and the only state I could think of between Ohio and California was Texas.

"Texas," I said. "To visit my aunt. They have a big ranch there."

"Really? Do they have cattle?"

"Uh, yeah, but I think oil wells too." The only thing I know about Texas is that James Dean's last movie, *Giant,* is about this big ranch in Texas where they discover oil. I can't wait for the movie to come out. James Dean was killed while he was working on it, so it's the last James Dean movie there'll ever be. Anyway, if I'd seen the movie already, maybe I would have known something more about Texas, but I hadn't.

"Oil wells. My, my."

I looked sideways at her. I don't know if she believed that part about oil wells. Maybe that wasn't such a good idea. Maybe she thought I was making it all up. Or maybe just bragging or exaggerating.

"Actually, I think just one oil well," I said. "I mean, they're not really rich or anything."

"It sounds exciting." She leaned her head back against the seat. "I think I'll just see if I can catch a little nap before we make our stop." She turned to look at me. "By the way, I'm Ruby Durban. Forgot to introduce myself." She held out her hand.

"I'm Venida Meredith," I said, hearing how it sounded for the first time. I shook her hand.

I wasn't positive I would keep that name, but there was time to change it again before I got my first part in the movies.

"What an interesting name. I don't think I've ever known anyone named Venida before." She settled back in her seat.

That was good. That meant my name would be unique and memorable. I picked it from a hair-net advertisement in a drugstore. I'd stopped to have a Coke after I bought my bus ticket and the sign was right there in the front window: VENIDA HAIR NETS. I thought it was a very interesting name.

I tried a lot of names with it while I was sipping at my Coke. Like Valli. I really liked Venida Valli, and the two same initials I thought was good, like Marilyn Monroe. Really eye-catching. Only there's a singer, June Valli, and I didn't want to get mixed up with her.

Then I thought since Venida was such an unusual name, I ought to have a sort of exotic last name to go with it, maybe a French-sounding one, like Darcel. But there's already an actress named Denise Darcel, so that was no good. Too bad, because I really liked Venida Darcel.

Finally I came up with Meredith, because it sounded kind of smooth and like a name a rich person would have. And I decided that if I had such an unusual first name, I wouldn't need an unusual last name too.

Mrs. Durban settled back in her seat again and closed her eyes.

I was glad. I didn't want to get too friendly with anyone because I figured the less people noticed me, the better. The bus was only half full and I hadn't spoken to anyone else besides Ruby Durban. I don't even know why she took that seat, since there were some empty ones, so she could have had a window seat, but maybe she got bored without being able to read and wanted to be near somebody to talk to.

I opened my movie magazine and began to read the article about Kim Novak and how almost everything in her house is lavender. It's her trademark, but I knew that already.

She said she wasn't ready to think about marriage yet, she was just starting on her career, and everybody had big hopes for her after *Picnic*.

"When I get married, it'll be for keeps," she said.

I shut the magazine. That's what I would say when they interviewed me for *Photoplay*. I feel exactly the way Kim Novak does about marriage.

When *I* get married, it'll be for *keeps*.

We stopped for supper at Sal's Roadside Rest in Medford, Pennsylvania. The driver told us we wouldn't stop after that until we were in Ohio, which would be in the middle of the night. The driver seemed to know the lady behind the counter, but he called her Winnie, not Sal, so I didn't know if she was the owner or just a waitress.

Everybody wanted to use the rest rooms, including me, so Winnie took all the orders and people waited in line to get to the bathroom.

The diner had counter seats and booths. I ordered a chopped-steak platter with French fries and lettuce and tomato, plus a Coke and a piece of apple pie and ice cream. Winnie said I ought to try their special, which was sweet-and-sour pot roast with noodles and cabbage, but that was $1.25 and the chopped steak was only 85¢. Since I didn't know how long it would take me to get a job in California, I figured I ought to be as thrifty as possible.

While I waited to get into the rest room, I noticed that there was a jukebox over in the corner, and even though I was "pinching pennies," I couldn't resist putting a nickel in to hear Elvis sing "Heartbreak Hotel." After all, I told myself, I had just saved all that money on food, so I could spend just a nickel to hear Elvis sing my favorite song. Who knew how long it would be until I got a radio?

The music blared out and I stood next to the jukebox and sort of swayed in time to the rhythm. I love the beat of that song, and it's hard to keep still with the *thump, thump, thump* of the guitar practically punching you in the stomach.

Winnie was putting plates of food on the counter and scowling. She looked over at me and shook her head. "I don't know how you can listen to that screecher," she said, talking over the music. "You know what Sal calls him?"

I wanted to listen to Elvis, not Winnie, since I had just spent one of my hard-earned nickels on him, so I just shook my head.

"Elvis the Pelvis." Her mouth twisted in a sort of sarcastic smile. "Isn't that something?"

I wonder if she thought Sal made up that nickname. I'd only heard it about three hundred times before. Probably two hundred of the times I heard it were when Uncle Ted was teasing me about liking Elvis.

I smiled, as if I really thought it was something, and kept tapping my hand against the side of the jukebox until the record was over.

I wished I could hear it again, but Winnie waved me over to the counter, holding my plate of food up for me to see.

I was so hungry I must have broken all the records at Sal's Roadside Rest for speedy eating. The chopped steak was like hamburger without a roll, but the apple pie was really delicious.

Mrs. Durban sat on one side of me at the counter. She was having the special sweet-and-sour pot roast and telling Winnie how good it was.

On the other side there was a woman with a baby in her arms, who had been sitting at the back of the bus. Winnie heated up the baby's bottle in a pot of water.

Everybody put tips down on the counter for Winnie, so I realized I had to too. Mrs. Durban put down two dimes. I hadn't figured on tips, and I realized then there might be a lot of extra little hidden expenses I hadn't figured on before this trip was over.

I went to use the rest room, and put on fresh lipstick and touched some pressed powder to my nose and chin. I really would have liked to put on all new makeup, but there was just this tiny mirror over the sink, and no counter to put stuff on, and the light wasn't even any good for makeup.

I reached for the envelope with the money in it, and decided I'd better keep it in my wallet. It would look pretty strange to take money out of an envelope every time I had to pay for something. I was just switching the money from the envelope into my wallet when the woman with the baby came into the bathroom. Only she didn't have the baby with her.

I quickly stuffed the wallet into my pocketbook.

"I'm sorry," the woman said. "I didn't know there was anyone in here."

"That's okay," I said. "I'm finished."

I wasn't sure, but I thought she was looking at me kind of suspiciously. I crumpled the empty envelope and tossed it into the metal trash bin under the roller towel. I tried to look casual about it, and I guessed it was okay, since she was already in the john and closing the door behind her.

Mrs. Durban was sitting at a booth, giving the baby its bottle. I paid Winnie for the food and put 20¢ down next to my plate when she was at the cash register.

"Five minutes, Venida," Mrs. Durban said. "We'll be leaving in five minutes."

"Okay. Thanks."

Five minutes was just long enough to play "I Was the One," which is the flip side of "Heartbreak Hotel" on the jukebox, but I decided that what with the extra expenses I hadn't counted on, I'd better not. I told Mrs. Durban I'd see her on the bus, and went outside.

I showed the bus driver my ticket and he nodded and I went back to our seat. I'd left my movie magazine on it, and my hatbox was in the rack right over it. I sat on the aisle seat until Mrs. Durban came onto the bus. She insisted that it was my turn to take the window.

"It's pretty country around here," she said. "You'll see some nice farmland. It's going to be dark pretty soon anyway, so we might as well not change seats anymore."

It was pretty. We passed a lot of farms, all flat and stretching out for miles, but with mountains way beyond in the distance. I even saw some horses and a couple of windmills, which didn't look anything at all like the pictures of windmills in Holland you always see.

It all looked so peaceful and quiet, and private, so different from Robin Lane, where rows of houses were practically rubbing up against each other so that when you looked out your bedroom window you looked right into your neighbor's bedroom window.

I wondered what it would be like to live on a farm, to live someplace where when you looked out your window you saw cows and horses and mountains and fields like checkerboards, brown dirt, then green, then gold, then brown dirt again. And all that space, all that privacy, to do whatever you wanted without anyone around to watch you, without anyone you had to talk to just because they happened to be in their backyard at the same time you were in your backyard.

I thought it must be very peaceful.

I knew Hollywood would certainly not be anything

like that, but I thought, maybe if I really made it big, I could afford to buy myself a farm. I know there are plenty of farms in California, plus ranches and orange groves, etc., and maybe I could buy a farm and go there for weekends, or between movies or something. That would be where I could rest and be alone, away from the "hurly-burly" of the movie business, and the pressure of fans always following me around trying to get my autograph.

Of course, I didn't think I would find "autograph hounds" too hard to take. I thought it would probably be a long time before I got tired of them. Like William Holden says, "It's when they *stop* asking you for your autograph that it should bother you."

But being a movie actress is hard work, like getting up at six A.M. or even earlier and working till five or six at night. It really isn't all glamour and premieres and movie-magazine interviews. I'm not kidding myself about *that*. So I probably would need a nice, quiet place to "get away from it all," and a farm might be just the thing.

It would be a great place to do magazine stories, too. Lots of good picture possibilities: riding my horse around the farm, or milking a cow, or maybe just leaning against one of those rail fences in a sunsuit, enjoying Nature.

It was getting dark. You could hardly see out the window now. Mrs. Durban had dozed off again beside me, her head tilted to one side. She didn't look very comfortable. I leaned against the window and closed my eyes.

Sometime in the middle of the night, I woke up and found we had stopped. Most of the lights in the bus were dim. I glanced out the window and saw we were in some sort of terminal or station or something, because there were other buses on either side of us.

Mrs. Durban was gone. This must be Springfield, where her son and grandchildren lived.

Now that I had the whole seat to myself, I was tempted to lie down. I could, if I scrunched myself up so that my knees were against my chest and my head right up against the window side, but I was afraid of ruining my dress. It had to last four more days, and I thought it must be getting creased enough just sitting on it all these hours.

And I was so tired I didn't seem to be having any trouble sleeping sitting up, so I just leaned my head against the window again and closed my eyes. I never even knew when the bus started up.

I woke up all cramped and achy. My neck felt stiff and my head was kind of fuzzy. It was really early in the morning, I could tell. The sun wasn't out all the way yet, and through my window the flat, empty miles of green seemed to be half in the shadows.

I had no idea where we were, but it was hot. This early, I thought, and already so hot. The bus was very quiet. Almost everybody was still sleeping, or at least not talking. I looked around and saw that the woman with the baby was gone. I guess she'd gotten off in Springfield too.

I looked toward the driver's seat and saw that the bus driver had different color hair. I realized the first driver must have finished his work for the day, and gotten off at Springfield, because, after all, how could one person drive all the way to California and go without sleeping for five days?

I didn't know when we were going to stop for breakfast, but I figured it couldn't be too soon, since it was still so early. I thought, I must look an absolute *fright;* I hadn't even washed my face since yesterday morning.

I stood up on shaky legs and stretched to reach my hatbox in the rack over my seat. I would put on all new makeup, check my hair, maybe dab a little cologne around my neck and chest, which might make me feel cooler.

I opened the hatbox and got out my round makeup mirror, which has one side magnifying and one side normal. I did look awful—especially on the magnifying side.

I wiped cold cream all over my face to get the old makeup off, and wiped it with tissue. All the stars use cold cream to take their makeup off, because they say soap is too harsh on the skin. But I like to wash my face with soap at least twice a day. Even though I don't have oily-type skin there is no point in asking for trouble.

I patted my neck and the part of my chest down to the top of my dress with tissues and splashed cologne on. A good thing to do in the summer to keep cool and help you stay fresh is to keep your cologne in the refrigerator, so it feels deliciously icy every time you dab it on your body, but of course, this was a Greyhound bus and there was no refrigerator to keep my cologne in.

So it didn't make me feel all that cool when I put it on, but I did feel fresher. I couldn't take a shower, of course, and the idea of not being able to take a shower for five days bothered me, but I decided that the minute we stopped for breakfast I would go into the rest room and at least wash under my arms and put on some more Mum.

My hair looked okay, except for my angel wings, which

were going a little limp in the heat, and the one on the right was sort of squashed from leaning against the window all night. But the French twist was okay as far as I could tell, with only some wisps coming down on the bottom against my neck.

It is not the easiest thing in the world to put on make-up in a moving bus, but with the extra room on the seat, I could at least spread out a little and take my time.

My friend Judy can put on lipstick in a moving bus without even looking at a mirror and I've never been able to understand how she does it. Every time I ask her she says, "I don't know, I guess I just know where my lips are."

Anyway, I managed, and trying to get my lipstick on in a moving bus, even with a mirror, made me think of Judy and how bad she was going to feel that I had gone off without saying good-bye, or even hinting about what I was going to do.

I don't have a whole lot of friends. I had to go to a new school when I moved in with Aunt Grace and Uncle Ted, and it takes a while to get to know people. And I was never sure I wanted people to get to know me all that well, because as far as I could tell, I was the only person who didn't have a mother and father, or at least *one* parent, and I didn't like the idea of everybody knowing I was a foster child and asking a whole lot of questions. Which they would if I got too friendly with them.

And besides, like I said, the kids in school are very immature. They don't have a goal like I do. They don't do anything with their lives but study and go to dances and go on dates and giggle about boys who are just as immature as they are. So we really don't have much in common.

But Judy knew about Aunt Grace and Uncle Ted taking me in right from the beginning, because she and her parents go to the same church, and they came over to meet me the first month I lived on Robin Lane.

Judy likes movies too, and we both kept scrapbooks and traded pictures that we didn't want for pictures we did want, except James Dean, because we both collect him. And even though she didn't know I was going to California now, she knew that I wanted to be a movie star, and she was sure I had the looks and talent to "make it big."

I could talk about *feelings* with her too, and she was the only person in the world I could do that with. Of course, I couldn't tell her everything, especially about Mr. Framer and Mr. O'Connor and definitely not about Uncle Ted, because she'd think I was really terrible, even if none of that was my fault.

But I could tell her other things about how I felt and what I dreamed of, and she would tell me her secrets, and I found there were lots of things I thought about and wondered about that couldn't have been so strange, because Judy had the same thoughts.

Anyway, that's why I felt really bad going off without a word to her, but when I wrote to her from Hollywood, after I was established, I knew she'd understand and forgive me.

Especially if I invited her out for a double date with Tab Hunter, who she thinks is absolutely fabulous!

I finished with my makeup and closed my hatbox with a sigh.

It was the best job I could do, considering.

The sun got brighter and hotter, and there were no more shadows on the grass. I began to see cows and more windmills and farmhouses back from the road. The barns were all red, just like the pictures of barns you see, only a couple of them had signs on the side, with a picture of an Indian girl and CALUMET BAKING POWDER painted on them. I thought that was very unusual, having an advertisement on a barn.

Finally we stopped.

There was a big sign that said SLEEPYLAND MOTEL AND RESTAURANT and a big parking space right in front of the restaurant part, with two round gas pumps next to the road. The motel part was stretched out behind the restaurant, this whole bunch of cabins that looked like they were made of logs, all connected in a sort of *U*-shape.

The driver got off the bus and said we'd have forty- five minutes to eat and do whatever we had to do. I took my hatbox with me because I wanted to do more "freshening up" in the bathroom.

When I got inside the restaurant, which also looked like a log cabin, only bigger than the motel rooms, there was a line that I knew must be for the rest rooms. I was glad I had put on makeup on the bus, even if I didn't do the greatest job in the world. I'd hate to have anyone see me looking like some of those women lined up for the bathrooms looked.

There was a red-headed lady behind the counter taking orders. I ordered the special breakfast, which was hotcakes, juice, and coffee or milk. The waitress asked me if I wanted the deluxe, which came with sausage and was 20¢ extra, but I said no. Every penny counts, I reminded myself.

There were booths here too, and though there was no big jukebox, like in Sal's Roadside Rest, there were those new little ones right in the booths, with rows and rows of selections to choose from. I slid into a booth and flipped through the titles, not really meaning to play anything, just curious to see what records they had here. Wherever "here" was—I still didn't know.

When I saw they had Elvis's brand-new hit, "I Want You, I Need You, I Love You," I just couldn't resist. It had only been out for about a month, and I hadn't gotten to hear it too many times yet, and who knew when I'd get a chance to hear it again?

And besides, I'd saved 20¢ by not getting sausage with the pancakes, so I was still really being thrifty and saving 10¢ anyway, even though these new little jukeboxes cost a dime to play instead of a nickel.

I reached into my pocketbook to get a dime. I felt around, but there was so much stuff in there, I couldn't get to my wallet. I started taking things out and lining them up on the table: my compact, my lipstick, tissues, my pink scarf, the sunglasses with the white plastic frames I'd gotten at Woolworth's, my pad and pencil for letters to my mother and Judy.

Faster and faster I grabbed for things, and the more stuff I took out, the more frantic I got. I should have been able to get to the wallet by now. I should have been able to feel it in there. I didn't remember putting all this stuff on top of it anyway. I'd switched my money from the envelope to the wallet and paid Winnie for my supper from the wallet, and I didn't remember taking anything else out of my bag after that. So the wallet should have been right on top.

Except, it wasn't.

I stretched the bag all the way open and looked inside. My wallet was gone.

Chapter 5

For a moment I was so shocked that I just kept looking into the pocketbook and rummaging around, sure that my pink plastic wallet had to be there, even though I could see that it wasn't.

Then, the first thing I thought was, I better tell the waitress to cancel my breakfast because I couldn't pay for it. That was all I could think of, so I went up to the counter in a sort of daze and told her I changed my mind about breakfast, I wasn't really hungry. I think maybe she looked annoyed, but I'm not sure, I can't remember. All I know is I almost collapsed into the booth and sat there staring at the things I had taken out of my pocketbook.

After a few minutes I began putting my stuff back into my pocketbook slowly, one thing at a time, like if I did it carefully enough I would discover that one of those things was actually my wallet, that it wasn't gone at all, it had been there all the time, but I just hadn't noticed it.

Only, of course, it wasn't.

What was I going to do? I stared down the row of booths. There was a man in the booth at the end, facing me. He was eating breakfast and as I sat there, staring, he looked up and stopped eating for a minute, holding his fork right in front of his lips.

I shook my head, like I could clear away the fog that seemed to be in my mind.

What was I going to do? I didn't have one penny, not one

red cent, every bit of my $137 was gone, and not only that, but my bus ticket was in my wallet too.

Would they let me back on the bus without a ticket? Every time we got back on after a stop, we showed the driver our tickets. How else would he keep track of who was a paid passenger? Anyone could get on the bus, and the driver wouldn't know the difference unless he saw a ticket.

And this wasn't even the same bus driver we had yesterday. He wouldn't know I'd been on the bus all night, unless he'd noticed me, and I'd been keeping away from the other passengers, so they might not even be able to say, "Yes, I remember her, she was on the bus."

The only people who could swear I belonged on that bus were Ruby Durban and the woman with the baby, and they had gotten off at Springfield.

I thought my stomach would drop into my shoes. I remembered the woman coming into the rest room at Sal's, seeing me with all that money, seeing me put it in my wallet.

I had been asleep for hours before the bus stopped in Springfield. My pocketbook had been on my lap, but she could have just reached in and lifted the wallet. As far as I could remember, it had been right on top when we got out of Sal's Roadside Rest.

But she would have had to lean over Ruby Durban to do it, because I was sitting next to the window. And wouldn't someone have seen her?

Not if everyone on the bus was asleep.

Maybe Mrs. Durban had taken it. It would have been easy for her. She was sitting right next to me, she could have waited until I fell asleep. . . . But a nice old lady like that? I couldn't believe it.

Maybe she believed the story about my aunt and uncle having a big ranch and oil wells. Maybe she needed the money and thought I was so rich I wouldn't even think twice about losing $50. I was all dressed up, I was carrying my model's hatbox, I looked like I could be a rich girl, I guess.

But I still couldn't believe it. Women with little babies in their arms aren't pickpockets. That nice Ruby Durban, with her son working at Sears, Roebuck and her little twin grandsons, couldn't be a thief. Maybe I had lost it. Maybe it had dropped on the floor under my seat.

I jumped up and ran outside and climbed on the bus. I went back to my seat, squatted down, and felt all around.

No wallet.

I looked up and down the center aisle. I started looking under every seat, but it was no use, I knew that. The wallet wasn't on the bus. I went back into the Sleepyland Restaurant and slumped into the booth.

Either someone had stolen my wallet, or I had lost it somewhere between Sal's and here. Maybe even walking out of Sal's and onto the bus. But no, I remembered, I had shown the driver my ticket, put it back in my wallet, and put the wallet back in my pocketbook.

So someone had to have taken it.

But what difference did it make what had happened to my wallet? The main thing was, I was stranded in the middle of nowhere with no money and no bus ticket and *no one I could tell.* If I told the bus driver my wallet had been stolen, he would probably call the police. How could I ask the police to look for the person who had stolen my wallet, when the police were probably looking for *me?*

I put my head in my hands and tried not to break down and cry.

Even if the driver let me ride the rest of the way to California without seeing my ticket, what was I going to do once I got there? I couldn't expect to get right off the bus and walk to the gates of MGM and get a part in a movie just like that. I don't believe in fairy tales; like I said, I'm practical. And where would I live, how would I eat, how would I get around to the studios even if I got some other jobs modeling while I was waiting to break into pictures? It could be a week until I got my first paycheck; even if I started working the very first day in California, that would be five days with no place to sleep and no food to eat.

Three years of saving, three years of planning, and now everything was gone, my dream destroyed, not even twenty-four hours after I'd set out on my new life.

"Miss? Is anything wrong? May I be of assistance?"

I looked up and saw that the man from the back booth was leaning over, holding out a little white card. I didn't know what else to do, so I took the card. It had "Walter Murchison, Good News Publishing Co." printed on it.

"Whatever it is," he said gently, "it can't be that bad."

It *can* be that bad, I thought angrily, and almost said it out loud, but I stopped myself. I couldn't tell him the truth, if I didn't want to be caught, but on the other hand, he had a kind face, and a pleasant voice, and maybe he could help me if he knew it really *was* that bad.

If he knew why I was in such a jam, he'd probably go straight to the police, because he'd get in trouble if he helped me. And if he knew I was fifteen, he'd turn me in for sure and tell me he was doing it for my own good, because

I was too young to be running off on my own. But if I said the right combination of words maybe this Walter Murchison would save my life.

"Well," I began, my mind racing, "it's sort of a long story."

"Then may I sit down? I'd like to hear it."

I nodded. He had a kind face, not real handsome, but nice. His hair was very short and sort of sandy-colored and he wore a seersucker jacket with narrow blue and white stripes and a white shirt. He had a red bow tie, which I didn't like too much because I don't like bow ties, plus it sort of sat on his Adam's apple and made you notice how it stuck out.

But other than the bow tie and the short hair, he looked okay.

Even as I started talking I was trying to think up a good story, so I talked really slow, which was okay because he knew I was upset and he probably would figure I was having trouble getting the words out. Which I definitely was, but not for the reason he thought.

"I was on my way to Hollywood—I mean, I *am* on my way to Hollywood—"

"I knew it!" he said. "I took one look at you and said, 'That girl's a movie star or something. I'm sure I've seen her before.' You are a movie star, aren't you?"

"Well, no." I couldn't help being flattered, no matter how bad my situation was, because here was a complete stranger telling me I looked like a movie star. But it only felt good for a few seconds.

"Not yet, anyway," I said.

"You're going to be, is that it?"

"Right. See, the thing is, I'm on my way to Hollywood to be in the movies. . .

"Do you have a contract yet?"

"Well, no, not exactly." But that gave me an idea. "They wired me the money, though, for a screen test, and I quit my job and took the first bus I could get to California."

"Well, how in the world did you end up here in the middle of jerkwater Indiana?"

"Is that where this is?" I asked. "Jerkwater, Indiana?"

He laughed. I thought it was strange his Adam's apple didn't move when he laughed. I tried not to stare at it.

"No, that's just an expression. This place is called Dugan."

"Oh. Well, you see, I wasn't paying too much attention to where we were stopping, all I knew was I had to stay on to the last stop, which was Los Angeles."

Think, I told myself desperately. Plots of a dozen movies I had seen jumped around in my head, but none of them was any use to me. This was not the Lillian Roth story, or the Jane Froman story, or the Glenn Miller story, this was *my* story, the Sylvie Krail-Venida Meredith story, and no one had made a movie of it yet. I had to think it up myself.

"Well, I haven't a friend in the world, and I'm an orphan so I have no relatives either. . . ." Both those things were practically the truth, I realized.

"All alone?" He shook his head.

"That's right. So I really have no one to turn to in my time of need."

"And this is your time of need?"

I nodded.

"But, what happened?"

"Well, there was this old lady sitting next to me on the bus." Now I had it! I would tell him mostly the truth, just change it a little so he would see he really had to help me.

"And I befriended her and she told me she was really down on her luck and had spent her last few cents on a bus ticket to Springfield, Ohio, where she had some relatives who might help her out even though she hadn't seen them in years."

Walter nodded.

"Well, I felt sort of sorry for her, being so old and all, and having no money and not even being sure when she got to her relatives that they'd take her in, and I thought how awful it must be to be old and poor and have no place to go."

Walter nodded again understandingly.

"And I thought, here I am, only eighteen—" I glanced at Walter to see if he believed that I was eighteen. He didn't make any kind of face like he didn't believe it, so I went on.

"—only eighteen, with my whole life ahead of me and a career in the movies when I'd be making lots of money, and I ought to help this lady. So even though I only had a little bit of money left over from my ticket, just enough to live on for a little while in Hollywood, I thought, Syl—I mean, Venida, you ought to help this lady out. This lady can't wait for you to be a star and make lots of money, she needs money *now.*"

Walter looked very touched, I thought.

"So I took out my wallet and gave her twenty dollars. Which left me with thirty dollars to live on in Hollywood. She said she couldn't take it, she made a fuss, but she took it finally. She said how she was real grateful and would look for me in the movies. And then I fell asleep, and when I woke up we were in Springfield and she was gone."

"And so was your wallet," Walter finished.

"Right. And I was just trying to do a good deed. I can't believe that nice old lady would have robbed me, after I tried to help her. She must have been very desperate."

"Oh, my. It's plain you don't know the way of the world, Ven—what did you say your name was?"

"Venida. Venida Meredith."

"Lovely name. Well, it's just as plain as day, Venida, you're too trusting. That woman was probably a con artist. She made up that whole story to get your sympathy, and when you took out your wallet to give her money, she made sure to see exactly where you put it back, so she could pick your pocket."

"Oh, I was afraid that's what happened, but I really didn't want to believe it. I don't like to think bad thoughts about anyone, but I was asleep until we got to Springfield and ..." I sort of let my voice trail off. I don't know why, but I had this kind of instinct that Walter would feel much sorrier for me if I didn't act mean or angry about being robbed, but talked instead like I thought all people were good and kind and honest.

"And now," I went on, "here's my big chance, when I'm supposed to report for my screen test, and I haven't even got my bus ticket, because that was in my wallet too. And I don't know how I'm going to get to Hollywood in time for my test, and my whole career is finished before it even starts."

I put my head in my hands again. This time I didn't try to stop myself from crying, but for some reason, now that it would do some good, no tears would come. I felt a hand on my head.

"Tell you what, Miss Meredith. You'll get to Hollywood on time. You'll take that screen test, and I bet you'll do real well, too."

"But how? I have no bus ticket, no money—"

"I'm going to take you, that's how. In my brand-new Pontiac Star Chief Catalina. I want to do something to help you restore your faith in people. A thing like this, why, it could sour you on the world. Being so young and impressionable. It's not good to be too trusting of people, so they take advantage of you, but it's not good to be too distrusting either."

I was absolutely stunned. I stared at Walter, not believing what he was saying. He looked pleased as punch, as if it made him really happy to shock me like this.

"But—but—to drive me all the way to California from Dugan, Indiana?" I didn't know what to say. The most I'd hoped for was maybe a small loan, which I would pay back when I got my first job. But this! To be driven all the way to California in a brand-new Pontiac! Just like a *star*. I was so bowled over I said the first thing that popped into my head.

"Isn't that going to take you a little out of your way?"

Chapter 6

Walter was still laughing when we walked out to his car, which was parked in front of one of the Sleepy-land cabins.

"It's beautiful!" I said, running my hand along one of the tail fins. Two-tone blue, with white leather upholstery. "Does it have a radio?"

"It has everything," Walter said proudly. "Radio, heater, power steering, V-8 engine, automatic transmission, white-wall tires, dashboard clock, cigarette lighter—do you smoke, Miss Meredith?"

Remembering Natalie's interview, I said, "I'm trying to cut down."

"You should see it after it's washed and waxed," Walter went on. "It gets pretty dusty on these back roads. We'll get it washed before we hit L.A. Don't want you showing up for your screen test in a dirty car."

"Goodness, Mr. Murchison, even if this car is dirty, it sure beats a Greyhound bus."

"Well, I'm sure you'll be more comfortable than you would be on the bus, even if it takes a little longer. And if we're going to be traveling companions, you'd better start calling me Walter."

"All right, Walter. And you call me Venida." But what he'd said about it taking a little longer bothered me. Why should a slick new car like a Pontiac Star Chief Catalina take longer to get to California than a big, hulky bus?

"When do you have to report for your test?" Walter asked.

I didn't answer right away. If I said, for instance, four days, would he say, "Oh, well, we can't get there that fast. You better find another way"? But when I told him my story, I made it sound urgent, like the test was practically tomorrow. I just couldn't think of the right-sounding date. And I couldn't risk losing Walter. He was the answer to my prayers, my only hope of reaching Hollywood and starting my new life.

Besides, his card had read "Good News Publishing," so on top of everything, it sounded like he worked for a newspaper. What a break! He might even do a story on me, give me some publicity, so that when I walked into the studios they would already have heard of me. The right kind of publicity can "make or break" an up-and-coming star.

"See, the thing is," Walter said when I didn't answer, "there's some territory I ought to cover before we head west."

That sounded interesting. I never met a real newspaperman, and I know they lead very exciting lives. There was this show on television, *Big Town*, which was all about life on a big city newspaper. All kinds of things happened to Steve Wilson when he was tracking down an important story.

"Well," I said carefully, "you're being so nice, I wouldn't want you to miss a big story on account of me.

Walter had unlocked the car. He put my hatbox in the trunk and I slid into the front seat. The car was steaming hot. I could feel the heat from the leather seat right through the back of my dress.

He slammed the trunk shut and got into the driver's seat. He opened his window wide and started up the engine.

"Purrs like a kitten, doesn't it?" he said proudly as we backed out of the parking space.

I took some tissues out my pocketbook and patted my face and neck. It was so *hot*.

"It'll be cooler once we get going," he said. "Roll your window down, let some air in."

We drove around the gas pumps and I could see people getting back on the bus. For just a minute I wondered if I wasn't making a mistake, if I should talk to the driver and see if he'd let me on the bus even without a ticket. At least that way, I'd know I'd be in Los Angeles in three days even if I didn't have any money. I had no idea what Walter's "territory" was or how many stories he'd have to cover before we got to California, and I was beginning to think a little more clearly, for the first time since I discovered my wallet was gone.

I began to get a little nervous. I didn't know a thing about this Walter Murchison except that he had a kind face and was a newspaper reporter. And what did a kind face mean? Ruby Durban had seemed to be a nice old lady, and she had probably stolen my wallet. You couldn't tell what people were like from their faces. Or the way they talked.

But then Walter pulled out onto the blacktop and we were whizzing down the road with a breeze coming in the window and it was too late to turn back.

How did I know Walter would actually take me all the way to Los Angeles? In fact, now that I could think straight, it sounded crazy. Why should he? Why should he pick up a perfectly strange girl in a restaurant and offer to drive her all the way across country just like that?

Everybody always warns you about accepting rides with strange men, and I never had. Not that any strange man had ever offered me a ride before. But if he had, I wouldn't have gone. What if Walter was some kind of maniac, and had no intention of driving me to Los Angeles, but was right now looking for some deserted spot where he would stop the car and—

"What did you mean, you wouldn't want me to miss a big story on account of you?" Walter asked.

I was leaning right up against the door, sitting as far from him as I could. I realized I was shredding my tissue into little bits, and my fingers were shaking. I stuffed the tissue back into my pocketbook, hoping he hadn't noticed. If he was a maniac, I didn't want him to know I knew it. I knew from the movies I had seen that you had to be really careful with crazy people and never let on that you know they're crazy.

"Well," I said nervously, "you're a reporter, aren't you? Your card said 'Good News Publishing.' Isn't that your newspaper?"

Walter began to laugh. He laughed so hard I was sure he *was* a maniac, and I would have jumped out of that car on the spot if we hadn't been going about sixty miles an hour. I looked ahead to see if there was a place he'd have to slow down, but as far as I could see there was the long, two-lane stretch of black road.

"I sell Bibles," he said when he finally stopped laughing. "Printed by the Good News Publishing Company of Fort Wayne, Indiana."

A Bible salesman! At first I felt this kind of twinge of disappointment that he wasn't a reporter, and wouldn't be doing a story about me, or even taking me along while he tracked down corruption and crime, like Steve Wilson did, but then I breathed a deep sigh of relief.

After all, what could be safer than riding with a person who was in the Bible business? Maybe I shouldn't have gotten into a car with a strange man, but if I had to get into a car with *any* strange man, I was certainly lucky that I had picked Walter Murchison.

I began to relax a little. It didn't seem so crazy that a person who devoted his entire life to Bibles would want to do a good turn for a desperate girl stranded without a penny to her name. Especially since he believed my story about trying to do a good turn for somebody else. "Do unto others as you would have others do unto you." That's from the Bible. Walter probably lived by that rule, which is called the "Golden Rule," and that's why he was helping me out.

"So you thought I was a reporter," Walter chuckled. "That's a good one. I'll bet you're disappointed." He glanced over at me. "I'll bet you thought I might do a story about you."

"Well," I said uncomfortably, "there really isn't any reason to do a story about me yet. I haven't even had my screen test."

"When is that screen test?" he asked. "You never did say."

"How long will it take you to cover your territory?"

"I should be able to finish it up in two days, I guess. And even if I don't, I have to come back this way after dropping you in Los Angeles, so I can always cover any areas I missed on my way back to Fort Wayne."

"Oh, that's okay then. As long as I'm there by Monday."
I thought that would give Walter enough time to take two
days to work and still get us to California pretty quickly.

"Well, that's fine. Shouldn't be any problem. Depend-
ing on how much time we make, we might even have a
chance to stop off in Las Vegas. Ever been to Las Vegas?"

"No." The only thing I knew about Las Vegas was that
people gambled there. It was legal, and they had big gambling casinos that stayed open all night. Was Walter a gambler? How could he be if he was a Bible salesman? That
didn't seem right. And if he wasn't a gambler, why did he
want to stop off in Las Vegas?

"A lot of show people got started in Vegas," Walter said.
"You ought to see it. They have great shows in the hotels
there."

Walter sure wasn't talking like my idea of a person who
devoted his whole life to the Bible.

"Can I turn the radio on?" I asked. The more Walter
talked, the more I started getting nervous again.

"Sure." He flipped the switch. Some guy was singing:

> *Did you ever see a robin weep*
> *When leaves began to die?*
> *That means he's lost the will to live,*
> *I'm so lonesome I could cry.*

That didn't sound like any of the music we got on the
radio at home, and I was going to change the station to try
and find someone playing the Top Twenty-five, but Walter
was singing along with the radio as if he liked the music, so
I just sat back and listened.

When the song was over he said, "I feel like that sometimes. I'll bet you do too, being all alone in the world."

"Yes, I guess so," I said. "I guess everybody gets lonesome once in a while."

"Very true, very true, Venida. You can even get lonesome in a crowd, did you know that?"

I thought about how I felt sometimes in school, with all the kids around, the boys singing that dirty version of "Sylvie" at me, the girls all clustered together giggling and making plans for parties and things, and I knew exactly what he meant.

"You're absolutely right," I said. "In fact, sometimes you can be lonelier in a crowd than you would be if you were all by yourself."

"Truer words were never spoken," Walter said. He nodded. He looked almost sad. "This job I've got," Walter went on. "It can be real lonely. That's why I'm glad of your company. It's nice to have somebody intelligent to talk to on these long rides. Sometimes you can drive for hours—there's more driving then there is selling in these backwoods areas."

"Where exactly are we going?" I asked nervously. I didn't like the sound of "backwoods areas" at all.

"Down to Kentucky, then Arkansas. Soon's I hit my quota we'll shoot right across Oklahoma and pick up Route Sixty-six. That takes us clear to California—if we don't stop in Vegas."

"Won't that take a long time?" I asked, worried. "I mean, going through two states and stopping all the time?"

"Don't you worry, Venida. I'll see you get to your screen test with time to spare."

Another song came on the radio. It was the same singer, but this time he was singing about a cheating heart.

"Must be a regular Hank Williams festival," Walter said. He seemed very pleased. "You like Hank Williams?"

"I don't think I ever heard of him."

"Never heard of Hank Williams?" Walter sounded like he could hardly believe it. "Where were you raised?"

"New—Jersey." I'd almost said New York, but caught myself just in time. I still had to be careful about "covering my tracks," even though the police would probably never expect to find me riding around Arkansas in a Pontiac Star Chief Catalina. But just in case there was anything on the news about a girl missing from New York, Walter might not be suspicious if he thought I was from New Jersey.

"That Hank Williams really knew about life," Walter said. "This rock-and-roll music, you listen to it, it sounds like savages in a jungle. And the words don't mean anything, it's all gibberish. Now Hank Williams, his songs tell you about *life*. Real life. They speak to the heart. Why, these two songs alone practically tell my whole life story."

"Really?"

"You bet. The reason I'm so lonesome I could die is because I'm on the road all the time and I don't have a wife to come home to anymore. And the reason I don't have a wife to come home to anymore is because she had a cheating heart."

"You mean, you're divorced?"

"Yep, that's the sad truth. She got bored waiting around for me all those times I was out working hard, doing my job, trying to provide her with the good things in life. And I did, too. She had a washing machine and everything. Everything a woman could possibly want. But she said she never had any fun. Imagine that. I said, 'Lena, you think I'm having any fun? You think going all over the Ozarks for days on end, trying to make enough money to buy you everything any woman could want, is *fun*?'

"Not that it isn't interesting," he added hastily. He glanced at me to make sure I didn't misunderstand him. "Don't get me wrong, selling the Good Book, bringing the word of God to all these people who might never be able to read it otherwise, is very rewarding work. But it's work just the same. Well, she just up and left one day. Took our little daughter with her too. Haven't seen either of them since. She mailed me the divorce papers from Reno."

"You have a daughter?" He must be even older than I thought.

"Yep. She'd be four years old now. Prettiest thing you ever saw. Big blue eyes, blonde curls all over her head. Name's Penny. Haven't seen her since she was two."

"That's a shame," I said. "When I get married it'll be for keeps."

"That's right," Walter nodded. "That's the way it should be. I never wanted to break up. It was all Lena's doing."

We'd been driving through farm country, all flat and open. The breeze that came in the window was getting hotter and hotter. I began to feel hungry, and wondered if we'd ever get to anyplace with a store. Walter had had breakfast, but I hadn't. It could be hours before he stopped for lunch.

We passed a sign that looked promising. It said Winota—5 Mi.

"Is Winota a town?" I asked.

"Calls itself a town. It's hardly more than one street with a couple of stores on it."

"Well, Walter, I didn't have any breakfast and I haven't eaten anything since yesterday, so do you think—"

"Venida, why didn't you tell me? For heaven's sake, we better get you fed or you'll die of starvation. Might as well do a little selling there too, long as we're stopping. Least it won't be so far between customers. And listen, Venida, one thing. I'll introduce you as my daughter, okay?"

"But your daughter's four years old," I said, puzzled.

"These people don't know that. The thing is, see, here's this beautiful young girl traveling with me, and they don't know who she is, the easiest thing is to tell them you're my daughter. You know, a Bible salesman has to be above reproach. Why, back in Fort Wayne, they don't even know I'm divorced."

"Oh, sure, I see what you mean." I wasn't sure I liked the idea. It sounded sort of sneaky, and I didn't know if a Bible salesman ought to be telling lies like that, but, after all, who was I to say? I'd told Walter a few tiny white lies because it was absolutely necessary, and it wouldn't hurt anyone to think I was Walter's daughter, would it? And it wasn't as if we were actually doing anything wrong by traveling together.

Because now I was pretty sure Walter was on the up and up, just by the way he was talking and not trying anything funny, so the whole thing was perfectly innocent. And if it was important to his job, why not? He was certainly putting himself out to help me; the least I could do to repay him was to go along with this one little white lie.

"All right," I said. "I guess I better practice calling you Daddy."

Walter laughed.

But you know, a funny little feeling went through me when I said that. It was the first time in my life I'd ever called anyone "Daddy."

Chapter 7

ISELY'S GENERAL STORE, the sign said. IKE ISELY, PROP. It
looked just like a store in a western movie. You had to walk
up the steps to a porch with a wooden floor and there was
even a guy sitting on the porch, tilting his chair back so the
two front legs were raised. He was wearing dungaree overalls and a straw hat, and if he'd been whittling or chewing
tobacco or something, he would have looked just like Gab-
by Hayes or Fuzzy Knight, except he didn't have a beard.

The heat hit me like a ton of bricks the minute we got
out of the car. It was like a baker's oven in that sun, and
there wasn't even a breeze to stir the air around a little like
when we were driving in the car.

It was hardly a bit better in the shade of the porch, but
right by the screen door there was a big red cooler with
COCA COLA written on it, and just thinking of holding an
icy bottle against my forehead made me feel a little better.

"Morning," Walter said to the man on the chair. The
man sort of grunted at him.

"Can't believe it's only seventy-five degrees," Walter
said. He pointed to a big thermometer over the cooler.
JOHN DEERE was printed at the top of the thermometer
and there was a picture of a deer on the bottom.

The man didn't even look up. "It's broke," he mumbled.

"I'm absolutely *parched*," I said, and for a minute I had
this spooky feeling that I didn't sound like myself at all. But
then it was okay, because I realized I was imitating Vivien

Leigh in *A Streetcar Named Desire*, which was a great movie, even though I saw it when I was only eleven, so I'm not sure I understood all of it.

"Absolutely parched," I repeated, just to hear the way it sounded again. I was really pleased. I never realized I could do a Southern accent. That would be a big help in my career, if I could do accents. Especially Southern accents, because there are a lot of movies made about the South.

"Get yourself a Coke and get me a Mission Orange," Walter said, "and come on inside."

"Thanks, Wal—*Daddy*." Boy, that felt strange!

Walter winked at me and went inside the store.

I opened the cooler and took out a Coke and a Mission Orange. I wanted to leave the top of the cooler off and just stand there, feeling the cold come up from deep inside and hit me in the face, but I didn't. Ike Isely might not like all his soda bottles getting warm, so I just took out the sodas, opened them on the bottle opener, and went into the store.

I never saw so many things crammed into one small space in my life. Isely's had everything from Uneeda Biscuits to undershirts. I couldn't figure out how he could manage to fit sewing thread, axes, lipstick, candy, electric fans, razor blades, laundry baskets, teddy bears, nightgowns, Carter's Little Liver Pills, blankets, saws, straw hats, and a ton of other things I could hardly keep track of, all in that little store, along with a whole line of groceries.

Then I thought, Well, Winota is such a small town, maybe he doesn't have to keep a whole lot of each item, just one or two of everything, so that probably saves space.

Walter was talking with a man with a round, red face and no hair who was standing behind a counter with a cash register on it. There was hardly any space on the counter to put things down. I went over to them and handed Walter his soda.

"Here, Daddy." I hoped Walter noticed how careful I was being.

"Thanks, honey." He tilted his head back and took a long swig of soda. I couldn't help staring at the way his Adam's apple bobbed up and down as he swallowed. Then I reminded myself I shouldn't stare at it, because after all, if I was supposed to be his daughter I'd seen his Adam's apple all my life.

Walter wiped his lips. "Very pleasant town," he said, smiling at the man, who I guessed was Ike Isely. "Looks like a nice place to raise kids."

"Well, 'course it's no Kokomo or Terre Haute," Mr. Isely said, "but it's all we got. Kids don't stay on, though, like they used to. Guess by the time they graduate school they've had enough of farming. You know, how you gonna keep 'em down on the farm after they've seen Fort Wayne?"

Walter laughed out loud. "That's a good one!"

"You planning on settling down 'round here?"

"No, just passing through. My daughter here got hungry, so I thought we'd stop and get her something to eat. I'll tell you the truth, I've passed this place so many times and always meant to stop and look around, because I've seen a lot of places in my line of work, but this is one of the prettiest patches of land from Fort Wayne to Little Rock."

"You don't say?" Ike Isely looked pleased. I wondered what he'd think if he knew what Walter had said about Winota five miles back.

"What line of work you in?"

"I spread the Good Word," Walter said proudly.

"You a preacher?"

"Nearest thing to one. Got a lot of godly people here?"

"As many as most places, I guess." I thought Ike looked a little suspicious.

"Well, as long as we're here, maybe I'll call on a few. Now, Venida, what would you like to eat? Looks like Mr. Isely has about anything a growing girl could want."

I'd finished my Coke and went to get another one while Ike cut up some ham to make me a sandwich. Walter was paying him when I went back inside.

Ike Isely was grinning at Walter and saying, ".. . hit most of them if you just follow down this road. They're none of them big spreads so it shouldn't take you too long." I guessed Walter had said something to make Mr. Isely less suspicious because he waved good-bye to us real friendly.

"Say," he called, as Walter opened the door to go out, "where did you get that dress?"

"May—" I'd started to say "Macy's" but I didn't know if they had any Macy's in Indiana, so I switched it really fast. "My Daddy got it for me in Fort Wayne."

"Sure is pretty. I'll bet if the girls around here could get dresses like that, they wouldn't leave home."

"Thank you," I said politely.

Walter gave me my ham sandwich and helped me into the car.

"That was quick thinking, Venida," he complimented me. "I heard how you started to say something else."

Walter started up the car and I tore into my ham, sandwich like I was starving, which I was. It was delicious. I held the Coke bottle against my forehead and neck when

I wasn't drinking from it, but the minute the bottle wasn't pressed against my skin I felt as hot as ever. Hotter even.

"I'll tell you what, though, Walter," I said. "I am just about perishing from this heat." I was still talking like Vivien Leigh. Who, by the way, is English, so it's really amazing she could play a Southern lady. I don't know why I kept talking that way, except maybe it was so hot I felt like I was in a movie about the South.

"I wish there was someplace I could change out of this dress into something cooler. I have nylons on and all these crinolines and I'm just about to die."

"Maybe you can change at one of the farms we stop at. Ask to use their bathroom, and take your bag in with you. Have you got anything to change into in that tiny little thing?"

"Nothing really decent, but in my suitcase—*my suitcase!*"

I completely forgot my Southern accent.

"My suitcase! Walter, I left my suitcase on the Greyhound bus!"

Chapter 8

"But everything I own is in that suitcase!" Half my sandwich lay on the seat next to me and I held the Coke bottle so tightly between my fingers I might have broken the thick glass. I wasn't drinking from it anymore. I was too upset to do anything but go on and on about my suitcase.

"Look, they must have a place for unclaimed luggage right at the bus terminal," Walter said. "First thing we hit Los Angeles, we'll find out where the Greyhound bus terminal is and we'll get your suitcase. It'll probably be waiting for you when we get there."

"What if somebody takes it?"

"Did they give you a baggage check?" Walter asked. "It was in my wallet!"

"Well, whoever took your wallet probably got off in Springfield, so the suitcase is still on the bus."

"Unless they showed my check and took the suitcase too."

"They probably didn't even notice the baggage check until they were off the bus," Walter said. "A pickpocket just wants cash anyway. They wouldn't bother with a young girl's suitcase. They wouldn't think there'd be anything of value in it."

We were pulling up in front of a white farmhouse set back from the road. I could hardly see through the tears in my eyes. "My scrapbook was in there," I said miserably. "That's valuable. To me, anyway."

"You had a scrapbook?" Walter sounded impressed. "You mean, with all your reviews and pictures and write-ups?"

"Sort of." I guessed I shouldn't tell him the scrapbook was full of pictures of *other* movie stars, and not of me. He might think—oh, I don't know what he might think. All I could think of was that besides not having a cent to my name, now I didn't own a thing in this world except the dress on my back, my three crinolines, and the stuff in my hatbox.

"Well, don't you see," Walter said excitedly, "that's great." He toned off the car and twisted around in the seat. "You can identify the contents of the suitcase. That scrapbook is your identification. No one else could claim that suitcase without describing your scrapbook, and only you know it's in there. All you have to do is tell them that, and they'll open the suitcase, and there'll be a book full of pictures of *you*. What more proof could they ask for, even without a baggage check?"

"Yes, I guess that's right." No need to tell him there were no pictures of me in the scrapbook. Once I got to Los Angeles, it wouldn't matter what Walter thought, and at least he'd given me some hope that I'd be able to get my stuff back.

"But what am I going to do until we get to Los Angeles?"

"We'll make plenty of stops along the way," Walter said. "If you need a few things, I'll be glad to buy them for you."

A woman had come out onto the porch of the house and was looking at Walter's car.

"I'll take care of you, Venida. Don't you worry about anything. Now, come on. I've got a customer to see."

I was beginning to think maybe Venida wasn't such a good name after all. Somehow I liked it less and less the more Walter said it. I don't know why. Maybe it looked better on the hair-net sign than it sounded when it was spoken out loud. I'm not sure. All I know is I thought maybe I ought to start thinking up some other names.

Walter got out of the car and went around to open the trunk. He pulled out my hatbox and a brown leather briefcase. He slammed the trunk shut and came to open the car door for me. He leaned in the window and said, "Now, don't ask to use the bathroom right off. Wait till I get her signature."

"Her signature?"

Walter opened the car door. "You'll know when," he said. "After she signs the paper."

I didn't know what he was talking about, but I didn't really care, either. I got out of the car and followed him up the dirt path to the house.

The woman was standing on the front steps with her arms folded across her chest. She wore a navy blue dress with red cherries on it and bedroom slippers without backs.

She didn't look like any farmer's wife I had ever seen; I'd never met a real farmer's wife, but I'd seen pictures of them, and in the movies, of course. Farmers' wives are all plump and jolly and they wear aprons all the time. She wasn't wearing any apron and she wasn't particularly plump and she definitely didn't look jolly.

"Do for you?" she asked, as Walter handed her his card.

"My name is Walter Murchison and this here's my daughter, Venida."

"You a salesman?" She turned the card over and over in

her hands. Then she looked at me, standing next to Walter, holding my hatbox, and seemed sort of confused.

"Well, ma'am, I don't like to think of myself as a salesman," Walter said. "The way I see it, I'm more of a messenger, like John the Baptist."

"That right? Well, whatever you call yourself, you're sellin' somethin' just the same, aren't you?"

"Eternal life, ma'am. Eternal life, that's what I'm selling. Nothing less."

She tilted her head to one side and squinted up her eyes, like she was trying to figure out what he meant. So was I.

"Mrs. Fitch—"

"How'd you know my name?" she asked.

"I don't claim to be Dunninger, ma'am. I didn't read your mind, I read it off your mailbox. Anyway, my girl and I have been driving three hours and it's mighty hot out here in the sun. If you could possibly—"

"Well, come on in then," she said impatiently. She opened the screen door for us. "Come into the kitchen, I'll get you something to drink."

"That's very hospitable of you, Mrs. Fitch. I can see I came to the right place."

Mrs. Fitch poured out two glasses of lemonade and handed them to us.

"You came to the right place for a glass of lemonade," she said. "But if you're looking to sell me anything, you came to the wrong place."

"But it's a nice place," Walter said. "Real nice. One of the prettiest spreads I've seen all the way from Fort Wayne to Little Rock."

I shot him a quick look, but he hadn't taken his eyes off Mrs. Fitch's face. He wasn't even drinking his lemonade, which was delicious. I'd already finished mine.

"It's a living," Mrs. Fitch said. "Barely. I have no extra money for fancy face creams, if that's what you're selling. It's too late for me to get eternal youth anyhow." She pointed to her face, which was creased with lines near her eyes and mouth. "See?"

"I'm not selling fancy face creams," Walter said gently. "And I know there's no such thing as eternal youth. I'm bringing you eternal *life.*"

He unbuckled his briefcase and pulled out a big, white book. He held it up in both hands so she could see it.

"This is the Holy Bible, Mrs. Fitch. The word of God. You don't need a fountain of youth when you've got life everlasting."

"We've got a Bible," Mrs. Fitch said. "What makes you think we need a Bible?"

"Of course you've got a Bible!" Walter cried. "Why, what would be the point of my even talking to you if you didn't have a Bible?"

Mrs. Fitch frowned. She looked really puzzled, which I could understand, because I was puzzled too. It sounded like Walter wouldn't try to sell a Bible except to someone who already had a Bible, and that didn't make any sense.

"Mrs. Fitch, let me explain with a parable, just like our Lord did. You're a farm woman, you'll understand what I mean when I tell you this. If you had two sons and the Lord gave you another son, would you say, 'Lord, why do I need another son? I've already got two'?"

" 'Course not," Mrs. Fitch said.

Walter nodded. "Is there a farmer in this whole, great country of ours that could ever have too many sons? The plowing, the milking, the sowing, the harvesting, the fence-mending—there's no end to a farmer's work."

"That's true." Mrs. Fitch nodded.

"And if you had one son that helped with the plowing and one son that did the milking, that doesn't mean you couldn't use another son to help mend the fences, fix the tractor, and keep all that expensive equipment in working order. It's the same with Bibles."

"How many Bibles does a person need?" Mrs. Fitch asked. "Bibles aren't the same as sons."

"But this Bible, Mrs. Fitch, is not the same as the Bible you already have." Walter held it up toward her again. "I'll bet your Bible is old and black and it's been in your family for years, isn't that right? And you've got all the marriages and births and deaths written down in it and—do you read your Bible, Mrs. Fitch?"

"Well, sometimes."

"In times of sorrow, or when you feel the need for a helping hand, or just want to feel closer to God. That's what most folks do. Good Christians, too, just like yourself. But to make a regular study of the Bible, to really know the Word of God, that isn't something most people do. I'll bet the print in your Bible's so small, you strain your eyes every time you try to read it."

"It is kind of small," Mrs. Fitch admitted.

"How can you study a Bible," Walter said seriously, "when the words are so tiny you get tired reading even a couple of verses? The Lord meant for his word to be *shouted*, Mrs. Fitch, not whispered."

He opened up the big, white Bible and handed it to her.

"Now, look at that. Look at the size of *those* words. God wouldn't have any trouble getting his message across to you with this Bible, Mrs. Fitch."

"My," she said, "I don't even need my reading glasses to see that."

"And you'll notice something else about this Bible too, besides simply the beauty of the white Leatherette binding and the gold stamping on the front. You see all that red printing in between the regular black print? That red printing is God's actual words. Every single word God speaks in the Bible, every single uttering of Jesus, is printed in red. You don't have to try and figure out the parts that are written by God and the parts that were written by the prophets and apostles. Why, the divine word of God just leaps out at you from every page."

Mrs. Fitch turned the pages of the book slowly. "It certainly is a handsome piece of work."

"All God's work is handsome," Walter said. "But if you don't mind a little humor, Mrs. Fitch, the Good News Bible is the *deluxe* edition of God's work. Now, tell me the truth. Isn't this a Bible you'd be proud to have in your home? Isn't this a Bible that wouldn't be stuck on a shelf somewhere, but would deserve a place of honor right out on a table in your front room? Please look at the gold-tipped pages too, Mrs. Fitch. This isn't just the holy word of God. If it isn't blasphemous to say so, a lot of people actually think of this as a decorative object, as well as a Bible."

I forgot how hot it was. I forgot my suitcase, my three scratchy crinolines, and changing my name to something other than Venida. I kept looking from Walter to Mrs.

Fitch and back to Walter again. This was like a Ping-Pong game and I couldn't figure out who was going to win.

"Mrs. Fitch, I know you're a busy woman. Your husband will be coming in soon for lunch, or you'll have to bring it to him." He held out his hand to take the Bible back. Mrs. Fitch looked like she didn't want to give it back, but she did. "So I'll ask you how much you think the word of God is worth."

"What do you mean?" she asked. "You want me to guess how much this Bible costs?"

"No. Just tell me how much the word of God is worth to you."

She looked confused. "Don't know. How can you put a price on God?"

"Exactly! The words of the Lord are like pearls beyond price. There just isn't any way to calculate the value of receiving the Good News. But what if the Lord said to you, 'My child, would you spend sixteen cents a day to hear what I have to say to you?' Imagine, Mrs. Fitch, sixteen cents a day to know the Lord! Sixteen cents a day to walk along the path of eternal life with Jesus! You wouldn't say, 'Well, Lord, we've had a lot of unexpected expenses this month, and farm prices being what they are, I think sixteen cents a day is a little high.' I just can't picture you saying that to the Lord, Mrs. Fitch."

Mrs. Fitch began to look the tiniest bit suspicious again. "Wouldn't say that to the *Lord*," she said, staring real hard at Walter. "What you're telling me is that Bible of yours is sixteen cents a day to buy, that right?"

Now I was sure Mrs. Fitch wasn't going to sign anything. I'd really been impressed listening to Walter and watching how Mrs. Fitch changed from distrusting him to being so interested in the way Walter talked, but I knew she was back to distrusting him again. I looked over at Walter to see if he knew she wasn't going to buy.

But he was just smiling gently. "Yes, ma'am. Sixteen cents a day. Less than it costs you to run your television set and worth so much more to you and your loved ones."

"Don't have a television set. Sixteen cents a day for how long?"

Walter opened his briefcase again. He took out a sheet of paper. "After the down payment, sixteen cents a day for five months."

Mrs. Fitch looked up at the ceiling and wrinkled her forehead. First I thought she might be praying to God, asking him whether she ought to buy this Bible or not, but then I realized she was trying to multiply in her head.

"It's right down here on the paper. The full price of the Deluxe Good News Bible is twenty-nine ninety-five. You put five dollars down and send us five dollars a month for five months. No extra charge for buying on time." He pushed the paper across the table so she could look at it.

"Five dollars down?" She frowned again.

"That's right." Walter took a pen out of his breast pocket. "And right there's where you sign, agreeing to pay the rest." He looked at his watch. "My, my, how late it's getting. Don't know if there's much point in stopping anywhere else."

Mrs. Fitch looked up from the paper.

"After all, Ike Isely told me, 'If you want to speak to the godliest person in town, you make sure and see Emma Fitch.'"

"Ike Isely said that?"

"Sure did. Said, 'If a good Christian woman like Emma Fitch doesn't want that Bible, you're sure not going to have much luck with the rest of the folks around here.'"

Mrs. Fitch reached for the pen, almost in slow motion. She looked sort of like she was hypnotized. I couldn't believe it. She scrawled her name on the bottom of the paper and handed it back to Walter.

"I'll get the five dollars," she said. I don't think Mrs. Fitch knew what hit her. I sure didn't.

After a couple of hours I realized that Walter was a really terrific salesman. We must have visited about ten farms all down the road from the Fitch place and Walter sold five Bibles.

I'd changed into my capri pants and a red-and-white-striped top at Mrs. Fitch's and Walter put my crinolines and my dress in the trunk of his car, wrapped in a blanket. I wanted to lay them out across the back seat, but Walter said it wouldn't look too good for a Bible salesman to be riding around with a pile of frilly lady's petticoats in the backseat of his car. He winked at me when he said that. I didn't think I liked the look of that wink at all.

At first it was kind of interesting listening to Walter talk to the different people and tell them different things to make them want to buy the Bible. He didn't just say the same stuff over and over again, except for that part about talking to Ike Isley. He told every woman that she was the godliest woman in Winota.

Another interesting thing was that when the farmers were home with their wives, Walter hardly sold a Bible at all.

"The women are the religious ones," he explained as we drove past the last farm in Winota. Walter had sold his fifth Bible there. "See how much easier it is when the husband isn't around? We should have taken the lunch hour off and waited for the men to go back to the fields. I'll bet we would have sold eight Bibles if there hadn't been any husbands around."

By now I was pretty tired of the whole business. It wasn't so interesting anymore. It was beginning to get boring. I was tired, hot, and starting to get hungry again. I was also beginning to wonder, since it took us almost two and a half hours to go about twelve miles, if we'd ever get to Los Angeles at this rate.

"Well," said Walter cheerfully, "I guess we've done enough selling for today. Better start making tracks. We can be in Kentucky before dark."

Something about what Walter said bothered me, but I wasn't sure what it was. I leaned back against the seat and sighed.

Walter turned on the radio and fiddled with the dial a moment. Then a man's voice came wailing out. Not the same one we'd heard before. This was a different singer.

I'm nobody's child, I'm nobody's child,
I'm like a flower just growing wild.
No mommy's kisses and no daddy's smile.
Nobody wants me, I'm nobody's child.

"Can't you get anything else on that radio?" I yelled. Those lyrics were really getting to me. I leaned over and punched one of the buttons. There was nothing but some crackling.

"You're just getting static, Venida," Walter said. He sounded hurt.

"Well, even static's better than that junk!" I settled back against the seat and closed my eyes.

"And my name isn't Venida."

Chapter 9

We stopped to eat supper at a Howard Johnson's. I felt kind of funny going to a restaurant in capri pants, even if it was only a Howard Johnson's, but it was all I had to wear, except for my dress, which was folded up in Walter's trunk.

We'd been on a main highway for a few hours and I'd apologized to Walter for snapping about the song on the radio.

"Oh, that's all right. I understand. I figured you were an orphan when you said you had no relatives. I guess they just hit you, those sad lyrics. That's what I meant when I said that music goes right to your heart."

Walter kept asking me, if my name wasn't Venida, what was it, and I kept saying I hadn't decided yet.

"My mystery lady," he chuckled.

By the time we sat down in the Howard Johnson's, I had just about decided on Lauri. There's an actress, Lori Nelson, but it's spelled differently, so I didn't think anyone would get us confused. I still liked Meredith, so I decided to keep that. I thought Lauri Meredith was a very nice name. I liked the way there was an "r" in both the first name and the last name, so that "Lauri Meredith" sort of rolled right off your tongue.

Walter told me to order anything I wanted. I remembered the night before, in Pennsylvania, where I had wanted the special dinner but was saving money for when I got to Hollywood. Now I wished I had gotten the expensive meal.

If I'd known my money was going to be stolen, I certainly wouldn't have bothered "pinching pennies" so the thief would find an extra 20¢ in my wallet.

I ordered a hot turkey sandwich with gravy and dressing and mashed potatoes. I was so hungry I was ready to eat the color picture on the menu.

"I'll pay you back for all this, Walter," I said, while we waited for the food. "As soon as I get a job. I'm going to take your address and send you every penny you spend on me."

"Now, don't you worry about that," Walter said. "Your pretty face and your company are worth more than I'll spend getting you to your screen test."

The waitress brought our food, and she hardly put the plate down in front of me before I was attacking it with my fork. Walter got the twin-knockwurst-and-beans plate. I was pushing the last bits of dressing around in the little smear of gravy left on my plate before he even finished one of his knockwurst.

I sipped at the last of my ice-cream soda and made a slurping noise with my straw. I looked around, embarrassed, to see if anyone had noticed. I pushed the glass away and sat back. For the first time in two days I felt like I'd had enough to eat.

"Would you like some dessert, Venida?" Walter asked.

"Well. . ."

"Oh, go ahead. I like to see a girl with a hearty appetite. Now, my wife, she was always dieting. She'd just pick, pick, pick at her food like a bird. And she was thin enough. I never could understand it. Go ahead. How about some chocolate layer cake?"

92

I certainly wouldn't be able to afford to eat like this my first few weeks in California. I thought I'd better get my nourishment while I could. But I really meant it about paying him back. I was going to keep a record of every penny he spent on me and send it to him just as soon as I earned some money. So far I owed him for the ham sandwich, two Cokes, the turkey, a black-and-white ice-cream soda, and a piece of chocolate cake. I'd make a list later on my pad.

Later!

That's when I realized what it was that Walter had said before in the car that bothered me. That thing I couldn't put my finger on.

"We can be in Kentucky before dark."

And then what? What did Walter plan to do when it got dark? He certainly couldn't drive all night and then spend the whole next day riding around selling Bibles. He had to get some sleep.

I looked across the table at Walter. He was just finishing the last of his beans. He'd taken off his bow tie and stuck it in his pocket, now that he wasn't working anymore.

" 'Bout ready to go, Venida?"

"It's Lauri." I fixed my eyes on his face.

"Say, that's nice. I like that even better than Venida. May take me a bit to get used to it though, after calling you Venida all this time. Why are you looking at me like that?"

"Just thinking."

He leaned across the table and grinned at me. "Penny for your thoughts."

If I'd had any money I'd have given a whole lot more than a penny to know what *he* was thinking.

I found out soon enough. About an hour later, just after it got dark, Walter stopped the car at the Traveler's Rest Motel, just outside Buford, Kentucky.

"Why are we stopping here?"

"We have to sleep, Ven—I mean, Lauri. I can't drive all night."

If sleeping was all he had on his mind, that was okay with me. But you couldn't blame me for being suspicious.

"You wait here and I'll register us." Walter opened his door and started to get out.

"Walter?"

"What is it?"

"You better ask for separate rooms."

"Separate rooms! Ven—I mean, Lauri—that's ridiculous. I'm traveling with you as my daughter. Getting separate rooms would just make people suspicious."

"Not getting separate rooms is going to make *me* suspicious, Walter."

"Of *me?*"

"I know it's going to cost you double, Walter, but I'll pay you back every penny like I said."

He scowled at me for a moment, then suddenly stopped scowling and smiled. "Okay. If that's how you want it."

He went inside the door that had OFFICE printed in lights over it and came back a couple of minutes later. He got back into the car, smiling. The Traveler's Rest, as far as I could see, was just a row of doors, each with a litde light over it. Walter started the car up again and drove down the row until he got to the space in front of the last door, farthest from the office. It had a number twelve on it.

"Here we are." He turned off the ignition and got out of the car.

"Is this my room?" I asked.

He pulled my hatbox and a small suitcase out of the trunk and slammed it shut.

"It's *our* room," he said.

I leaned out the window. "I told you to get separate rooms!"

"Keep your voice down!" he hissed at me. He came around to open my door. "They only had the one room. I tried, but this was all they had."

I looked around the parking lot. There were only two other cars parked in the whole place.

"I don't believe you! This place is practically empty!"

"It's still early. Some people are out eating and some have reservations and are coming later. This was all I could get. Now come on out of the car."

I didn't believe him and I didn't like the way he told me to get out of the car. I sat there, my arms folded, staring straight ahead.

He opened my door and leaned in to touch my arm. I yanked it away and slid over toward the driver's side.

"Don't touch me, Walter. I don't know what kind of a girl you think I am, but I'd rather sleep in this car than spend the night in a motel with a strange man."

"Lauri, I'm really hurt. What kind of a person do you think *I* am?"

"You're a salesman. Just like—someone I know." I was thinking of Uncle Ted. Even though he sold insurance and Walter sold Bibles, they were still both salesmen. And salesmen are people who can talk other people into buying things they might not really want. And Walter was a *very* good salesman.

"I can understand you not trusting people, after the experience you had," Walter said, his voice all soft and gentle, "but I thought you trusted *me*. After all, you came with me, you've been with me all day, you're going to be with me all the way to California. If you thought I was some kind of— well, you know what I mean—what would you be doing here in my car with me?"

I thought about that for a minute. It seemed to make sense. Even if Walter was fibbing about there being only the one room, it might be because he didn't want to spend the extra money for separate rooms. And I really couldn't blame him for that.

"Now, come on, honey. I'm dead tired and we want to get an early start tomorrow. The sooner we get going, the sooner we'll be in Hollywood."

I slid out of the car and slowly followed him to the door of number twelve. I reminded myself that I had had plenty of experience dealing with men. If Walter tried anything funny I could always scream. And I'd tell him so. The last thing a Bible salesman would want would be to have a girl screaming that he was attacking her in a motel room.

Walter opened the door and turned on the light. It was a little room, with pine furniture and two beds with green plaid spreads. I was relieved to see the two beds and I guess Walter noticed that right away.

"See, honey? Now, if I had designs on you, would I ask for twin beds?"

"You said this was the only room they had," I reminded him.

He looked sort of flustered for a minute. Then he cleared his throat and dropped his suitcase on one of the beds and my hatbox on the other. He walked to the bathroom and turned on the light.

"Nice and clean, isn't it? Nothing fancy, but they keep it clean."

I looked around. All there was in the room were the beds, a little chest of drawers with a mirror over it, and two lamp tables by the beds.

"Isn't there a television?"

"No. No air conditioning either, but it's cool now the sun's gone down. We don't really need the air conditioning at night."

"But no *television!* What else is there to do?"

"You could read," Walter said. "Or just take a shower and go to bed. That's what I'm going to do. You're probably tireder than you think."

I was tired, but not sleepy. And I certainly wanted to take a shower, if there was a lock on the bathroom door. But nine o'clock was too early to go to bed.

"I don't have anything to read," I said. "And I don't read much anyway."

"Why don't you take a shower and just cool yourself off and relax? You don't realize how tired you are. This traveling takes a lot out of you."

I sighed. What else was there to do but go to sleep? This was going to be some boring trip.

I unzipped my hatbox and pulled out my shampoo, cold cream, and my shortie pajamas. I remembered my flannel bathrobe, kicked under the bed back at the Tysons', and realized that I was going to have to wear those shortie pajamas in front of Walter. I didn't have a robe or anything to put over them. I never thought I'd need one again.

The only other thing I could think of was sleeping in my capri pants and striped shirt, but that wouldn't work out very well. I mean, I had to travel in those pants, I couldn't sleep in them too.

I didn't know what to do. I figured the only thing I could hope for was that if I told Walter to turn his back while I made a run from the bathroom to the bed, he wouldn't peek.

I went into the bathroom and checked right off that there was a lock on the door. I turned it, then got out of my clothes and unpinned my French twist. I shook my hair loose and ran my fingers through it, massaging my scalp. That's a very important thing to do before every shampoo. It stimulates the scalp and encourages healthy hair growth.

I wiped off my old makeup with cold cream and toilet tissues and stepped into the shower. I just stood under it with my face up to the warm water and thought, I'm washing away sweat and grime and tiredness from six different states! There was a scratchy white washcloth and I scrubbed myself all over with it. The soap was just a thin little cake of Ivory. I wished it was Camay, like I usually use, but beggars can't be choosers.

I shampooed my hair and rinsed it for a long time. That's the secret of a good shampoo. It's not how much lather you work up; the important thing is a good, thorough rinsing, to get all the traces of soap film off your hair. Most people don't realize that, but if you want shiny hair, rinsing until you can hear your hair strands squeak is an absolute must.

I dried myself off with the skimpy bath towel hanging on a rack next to the shower, and wrapped the other one around my head like a turban. It would take forever for my hair to dry. I'd probably have to sleep with it wet, which I don't like to do because my angel wings don't wave right unless I comb them and let them dry in place.

I slipped on my pajama top and the frilly little panties that go with it and took a deep breath. I unlocked the door, and suddenly got a great inspiration.

"Walter?" I stuck my head out the door. He was sitting on the bed, taking off his shoes. "Walter, we left my dress all bunched up in the trunk of the car. Would you get it out? I have to hang it up or it'll be a mess."

He looked a little irritated. "I just got my shoes off, Venida. Can't it wait till tomorrow?"

"It's going to be ruined, Walter. Please, I have to wear it for my screen test. I have to put it on a hanger. You can leave the crinolines in there if you want, but I really need to hang that dress up."

"Okay, okay," he grumbled. He put his shoes back on and went out to the car.

I made a dash for the bed, threw the bedspread back, and leaped in. I heard the trunk slam just as I pulled the sheet up over me. There was one thin, green blanket on the bed and I pushed that back with the bedspread because it was warm enough to sleep with just the sheet.

Walter came back into the room and shut the door. I think he was a little startled to see me already in bed.

"Here's your dress," he said. "It looks pretty creased. I don't know if just hanging it up is going to do much good."

"Would you please put it on a hanger for me?" I asked.

I wasn't going to get out from under that sheet till the next morning.

"Okay." He hung up the dress and sat back down on his bed, facing me. He took his shoes off again. "Feeling better now?"

"Oh, yes, much better. In fact, I think I'll go to sleep. You're right. I guess I was tireder than I realized."

"You going to sleep with that towel on your head?"

"Oh, no, I forgot. I have to comb my hair out. Would you get me my pocketbook, please?"

Walter got my pocketbook from the top of the chest and handed it to me. He was staring at me, looking puzzled.

"What's the matter?" I asked nervously. "Why are you looking at me like that?"

"I don't know," he said slowly. "You look—different. How old did you say you were?"

"Eighteen. Almost nineteen." I think I said it too loudly though. Like I was lying—which I was—and was trying to make him believe me by shouting.

"Boy, I don't know. You sure look different."

I toweled my hair and started combing it out. "It's the makeup," I said quickly. "That's why I look different. Because I washed all my makeup off." That was true. I look much younger without my makeup. I should have thought of that before. But I couldn't go for three or four days without ever washing my face, could I? That's the surest way to ruin your skin, going to bed with old makeup on.

"I thought makeup was supposed to make you look younger, not older," he said.

"It does for older women," I said. "It works the other way for younger women." I don't know how I thought that up, right on the "spur of the moment" like that. I was just trying to come up with something that would make Walter less suspicious, but as it turned out, that was a very true thing I said. Makeup does work that way. I wonder if anyone else ever thought of that?

I parted my hair in the middle and combed the angel wings in place, doing the best I could without a mirror. I certainly didn't want to get out of bed and stand in front of the dresser with Walter right there.

Before I realized it, the sheet had slid down so the top of my pajamas showed. I grabbed at it, to pull it back up over me, but Walter had already taken a good, long look.

"Yep," he said thoughtfully. "I guess you're eighteen all right."

I didn't like the tone of his voice at all. A little shiver went through me. I covered myself up again, but he was still standing there, staring, as if he could see right through the sheet. Or wished he could.

"Walter," I said, trying to sound real cold and firm, "if you come near me, I'll scream. Good and loud. And you won't sell a whole lot of Bibles around Buford, Kentucky."

He seemed to snap back, like he was just coming out of a trance. "For heaven's sake, Venida, you going to shoot me because I like looking at a pretty girl? You're going to be a movie star. You better get used to men appreciating your—attributes."

"Yes, well, you just better remember to appreciate my 'attributes' from a distance, Walter. And it's Lauri, not Venida. Now I'm going to sleep, so please turn off the light."

I spread the towel out on the pillow and lay back on it. I closed my eyes, even though I really wanted to keep them open so I could watch what Walter was doing.

He turned off the lamp next to my bed. He should have walked away then, but I didn't hear him move. I opened my eyes. The bathroom light was still on, shining into the room and making a big rectangle on the floor.

Walter was standing over my bed, looking down at me. My heart began to thud, just like he was Uncle Ted and I was back on Robin Lane.

"Why are you looking at me like that? Why don't you go take your shower and leave me alone?"

"I can't help looking at you," he said softly. "Ven—I mean, Lauri, you're the prettiest little thing I've ever seen. Don't be so distrustful of me. I won't hurt you. I'd never hurt you."

He sounded so sincere, and so hurt, that I almost felt sorry for him. Maybe I was too distrusting. He was spending money on me, going all the way across the country and out of his way to help me, and I was acting sulky and snippy. He'd said all he wanted was my companionship, and what kind of a companion was I being?

He reached over and touched my cheek. I started to freeze up, but his hand was so gentle that I just breathed out a sigh of relief and closed my eyes. Then I felt his breath on my cheek, and his lips brushed against it for just an instant.

My eyes flew open, but he was already on his feet and walking toward the bathroom.

I closed my eyes again. The soft night air drifted in the open window, and soon the room was filled with a smell much sweeter than Camay soap.

Chapter 10

"Pretty country, isn't it, Venida?"

I had given up correcting Walter every time he called me Venida. Sometimes he remembered and called me Lauri, but he said it was too hard to unlearn the name I'd first told him, so he kept calling me mostly Venida or just honey.

"Bet New Jersey doesn't look anything like this."

I didn't know what New Jersey looked like, since all I'd seen of it was a few glimpses out of the window of the Greyhound bus when I'd looked up from my movie magazine, but I'd told Walter that's where I came from, so I just said, "It sure doesn't." That was okay, though, since Walter didn't know what New Jersey looked like either.

It was pretty country. We'd been driving for hours, up and down hills, over narrow dirt roads just wide enough for the Pontiac to get through between the trees, and on strips of blacktop that looked like ribbon twisting through miles and miles of green mountains.

But the houses weren't pretty.

I'd see them from a distance, little dots on the sides of hills, like enchanted cottages plunk in the middle of shady forests, and I'd think, Maybe I won't get a farm after I get into pictures. Maybe I'll buy a little house in the woods.

And then we'd get close and Walter would inch the car up the dirt hill till he stopped in front of the house and I would see it wasn't an enchanted cottage at all. It was hardly more than a shack, all sagging and rickety and looking like it might tilt over and fall down the hill.

I went into the first few houses Walter called at, but after about an hour, I stopped going inside with him and just waited in the car.

These people were *poor*. I never knew there were such poor people in America. I never saw them on television. I couldn't remember any movies about people like this.

The women wore dresses or skirts that looked like sacks, with plaid shirts over them. Some of them had missing teeth and you could see black spaces when they smiled, but they hardly ever smiled. They were mostly pretty unfriendly. They looked at Walter and me like we were there to rob them or something.

Not that they had anything to rob. What they had mostly was children. All ages, all sizes, all skinny. In an hour of going into those houses, I didn't see one fat child. I also didn't see one child wearing shoes, which really shocked me. It was much cooler here than in Indiana, and the floors of the houses were all this rough wood, and you'd think you'd get splinters every time you put your foot down. I realized they weren't going barefoot because it was a hot summer day and they wanted to, but because they just didn't own any shoes.

I didn't see any television sets either, or washing machines or gas stoves or even toys except for some rag dolls. One little boy dressed in dungarees held up by a piece of clothesline for a belt was sitting in the dirt in front of his house dropping pebbles into a rusty old tin can.

I didn't see one book, one magazine, not even a movie magazine or *True Confessions*—not anything with printing in it except, once in a while, the Sears, Roebuck catalogue. I couldn't figure out why they'd even have that, since they probably couldn't afford to buy anything in it, but I thought maybe the children liked to look at the pictures and pretend they were going to get some of the things for Christmas.

Where were these people going to get $29.95 for a Bible, I wondered? How did Walter expect them even to have the $5 down payment? Their kids didn't even have shoes, and you could get a pair of perfectly good shoes at Miles or National for $4.98, so it seemed to me that if any of these people had $5 in the house, they had lots better things to do with it than give it to Walter.

Anyway, I started getting really depressed after the first few calls, and listening to Walter trying to convince the women that they needed a gold-stamped Bible more than they needed milk for their babies was getting on my nerves.

It had been interesting yesterday, when it was like watching a Ping-Pong game, following the ball bouncing back and forth over the net, wondering who was going to miss. Like with Mrs. Fitch, just when I thought Walter had missed the ball and wasn't going to get her to buy the Bible, he said something that made her change her mind, and he won.

But today I found I was rooting for Walter to lose. I didn't want him to be a good salesman, I didn't want him to be able to keep hitting the ball back. I wanted him to miss, to come out of every one of those houses with nothing in his pockets but the money he went in with.

So that's when I started waiting in the car.

About one o'clock we stopped at a house that didn't look as bad as the others I'd seen. Walter had been doing pretty badly and I was trying not to show how glad I was that he'd sold only one Bible in four hours. So he was really discouraged by this time. But when we pulled up in front of the last house, he perked up a little.

The house didn't look as rickety as most of the others we had seen, and if the paint wasn't new, at least it covered the wood, and wasn't all bumping and peeling.

A man in dungaree overalls came out on the porch with a shotgun in his hand. We'd seen plenty of guns at all the other places we stopped, so I didn't worry anymore when I saw someone carrying one. It seemed to be as ordinary around here as carrying a rolled-up newspaper was in New York City.

"I'll bet these people can read," Walter said, getting out of the car.

"I hope so," I said tiredly.

That was another thing that really threw me. Half of the people Walter called on *couldn't even read*. I mean, not the children, the grownups. Sure, I'd seen movies with real old Negro people who had been slaves before the Civil War, and they had to sign something and they said they couldn't read or write, so they just made an "X" on the paper, but that was only in the movies.

Walter got out of the car with his briefcase. He walked up the steps to the man with the gun and said something to him. The man propped the gun up next to the front door and they went inside.

I leaned back against the seat and closed my eyes. I was going to have to do something about getting Walter out of Kentucky and on the way to California before I went crazy. I couldn't take much more of this. The thought of two days of it before we started west was unbearable. If I couldn't convince Walter to get going, I'd ask him to lend me the money to take a bus. Even if I got to Hollywood with nothing but my hatbox, at least it would be Hollywood, and not Buford, Kentucky.

I heard a dog bark and opened my eyes. A tall, blond man was coming around the side of the house toward the car. He was wearing bib dungarees, like the other man, with no shirt, and, of course, carrying a shotgun. Then this big gray dog charged toward the car, barking.

We'd seen a lot of dogs that morning too, and they all barked at us, but I was still nervous every time one rushed toward me. I slid over to the middle of the seat, because this one looked big enough to stand up and stick his head inside the window.

"Hush, Duke!"

The man in overalls came right up to the car and I saw he wasn't a man at all, just a boy, but really tall. His blond hair was long and kept falling over his eyes.

The dog sat down next to the car and panted, his tongue hanging out of his mouth. He didn't look particularly mean or dangerous, just big, but I stayed in the middle of the front seat, just in case.

"Ain't seen you before," the boy said, bending down to look in at me.

"I've never been here before," I said nervously. "I'm just waiting for my—father. He's inside."

"Don't get many visitors."

"Well, he's not a visitor exactly. He's a salesman."

"Don't get many of them either. Why'n't you come on out of that car and stretch your legs?"

I looked at the dog. He was still sitting there, panting and watching me, like he was waiting for me to make a move.

"Oh, don't worry none about Duke," the boy said. He picked up a stick and threw it toward the side of the house. "Fetch, Duke!"

Duke went tearing off in the direction of the stick and the boy opened the car door and made a motion for me to come out.

Just as I slid out, Duke came running back and dropped the stick at our feet. I backed against the car, wishing I was still inside, and the boy laughed.

"He won't hurt you. Look, you throw the stick for him." He picked it up and handed it to me. I threw it as far as I could, which wasn't very far, and Duke bounded off again after it.

When Duke came back with the stick, the boy told him to lie down, and he did, and began chewing on the stick. I relaxed a little when I saw that Duke would just as soon chew the stick as me, and took a good look at the boy in the overalls.

He was really cute, even though he was so tall I practically had to strain my neck to look up at him. He was good-looking enough to be in the movies—sort of a cross between Burt Lancaster and Tab Hunter—ralthough of course I didn't know whether he had any talent or not. He was sort of cradling the gun in his arms like a baby and staring at me.

"Name's Jim," he said finally. "What's yours?"

"Lauri. Lauri Meredith."

"Pretty name."

"Thanks."

"Where you from?"

"Uh—Indiana." I figured I'd better say the same place that Walter was from, and then I realized I'd made a mistake saying my last name was Meredith when Walter's was Murchison, but it was too late to do anything about that.

I was feeling sort of flustered with this boy towering over me, staring at me like he'd never seen a girl before in his life.

Suddenly I wondered what it would feel like if he kissed me.

I don't know why that thought popped into my head like that, except maybe because no boy had ever kissed me. I was so embarrassed, like he might have read my mind or something, that I felt my face turning all hot and red. I never have thoughts like that about real people. I mean, people I know. Well, there is one person—but I can't talk about that. I've imagined James Dean kissing me, of course, and Harry Belafonte and other movie stars. I've watched hundreds of love scenes, and always wished there was some *real* boy who would kiss me and make me want to kiss him back.

Then I began thinking that if he did try and kiss me, he'd either have to practically bend himself in half to reach my lips or pick me up in his arms so I could reach *his* lips, and I knew my face was getting redder and redder.

I turned away and looked off toward the road. I felt a light tug on my pony tail and heard him mutter, "Pretty hair."

My legs suddenly felt weak, like I had to sit down, but I told myself that was because of all the sitting I'd been doing in the car, and the best thing would be to move around a little.

So I walked away from the car, toward the road, forcing myself to walk real casual, not like I was trying to get away from him or anything, just like I was exercising my legs to get the tiredness out of them.

I couldn't decide whether I wanted him to follow me, or to turn around and go back behind the house again, but I could hear his footsteps right behind me so it didn't matter which I wanted.

I didn't know what was happening to me, but it scared me. And it made my legs so weak that I knew walking wasn't going to help and I wasn't even sure I could walk steadily anymore. The only thing I knew was that I had this exact same feeling when James Dean kissed Julie Harris in *East of Eden*, and I sat there in the dark with my heart aching and wishing it was me instead of Julie Harris.

I leaned against the trunk of a big tree and closed my eyes. I didn't want to look at him, I didn't want to see him looking at me, I just wanted this feeling to go away so I could be normal again, with all my wits about me, and concentrate on the really important things I had to worry about, like getting Walter to start for California.

But the feeling didn't go away, and neither did he. Without even opening my eyes I knew he was right under the tree with me. I could feel the closeness of him, hear his breath, feel the movement of the air, and I knew he was raising his arms.

I opened my eyes. He wasn't holding the gun anymore. He had his hands on either side of the tree trunk just level with my head. His body was only inches from mine, but he wasn't moving it any closer, he was just standing there, surrounding me with himself, with his hands, trapping me against the tree.

Only I wasn't really trapped. I could have ducked out from under his arms without any trouble at all. He wasn't smothering me or grabbing me like Mr. O'Connor had, and I wasn't frightened of him, like I had been of Mr. O'Connor. I was frightened of myself, of what I was feeling, of knowing that I didn't *want* to duck out from under his arms.

I looked into his eyes. He was frowning, his eyebrows all scrunched like he was trying to figure something out. Then, suddenly, his arms went around the tree trunk and his body was pressing against mine. My hands were pinned to my sides, my cheek pressed against his chest.

My heart began to hammer so hard I thought I was going to faint. I twisted my head, gasping for breath, and felt the bark of the tree trunk scraping right through my clothes. I shut my eyes tightly, waiting for him to kiss me, sure he would now, and wanting it more than I'd wanted anything in my life.

Then, crazily, I thought of my other favorite scene in *East of Eden*. James Dean and Julie Harris are under this big willow tree, and you can't see anything but their legs because of the willow leaves hiding them, but you can imagine what's happening. And all the while I was waiting for Jim to kiss me, I was picturing this scene and feeling like he was James Dean and I was Julie Harris, and it was happening just like it did in the movie.

It was like one part of me could stand back and watch this scene while the other part of me was living it and growing dizzy with the feelings churning around in my body.

"JIM!"

"God-*damn.*" Suddenly the weight of his body was off me. I opened my eyes, dazed and confused. He was already walking away, back toward the car, where Walter and the other man were standing. I leaned there against the tree for a moment, too shaken to move, not sure that I'd be able to walk even if I tried.

He didn't even turn around to look at me. It was like it never happened, except that my heart was still pounding and I could almost feel ridges in my back where he'd pressed me against the tree.

I took a few deep breaths and slowly started walking toward the car. I don't even think my eyes were focusing very well, I was so shook up. Not only because of what Jim did, but because of what he didn't do.

When I got back to the car, Walter was scowling at me, and the other man, Jim's father, I guess, was apologizing to Walter.

"I know somebody's goin' to make good use of that Bible," he said angrily. "Maybe it's a good thing you happened by today, Mr. Murchison. Though I'm real sorry about the way my boy acted."

"To err is human," Walter said, "to forgive, divine." But he didn't sound very forgiving.

"Well, that's real Christian of you, Mr. Murchison. It'd been my daughter and somebody else's boy, don't know if *I'd* be that forgiving."

Jim just stood there, his back to all of us, looking off toward the woods. I couldn't believe he wasn't even going to turn around and say good-bye to me.

"You get on in the house," the man said. "I want to talk to you."

He never turned around. He just walked up the steps to the house with Duke at his heels, and went inside, slamming the door behind him.

I felt sick.

I grabbed at the handle of the car door. I slid into the front seat and stared straight ahead, waiting for Walter to finish talking to Jim's father. I didn't hear anything they said. All I could think of was Jim's body pressing against mine, how we'd been like James Dean and Julie Harris, and the way he'd turned his back on me and walked off like I never even existed.

Walter got into the car, slamming the door shut. He punched the starter and twisted the wheel to turn around.

He didn't say a word till we were back on the blacktop road.

And then he said plenty.

Chapter 11

"That was a pretty sight, Venida. You and that hillbilly trash humping up against the tree like that." Walter was crouched over the steering wheel, driving so fast that we dipped down hills like we were on a roller coaster.

"Never laid eyes on him in your life and you're letting him paw you like some kind of—"

"I didn't let him, Walter." I didn't care whether he believed me or not. "He just did it."

"He just *did* it," Walter mimicked me. "He just *did* it. He attacked you, is that it?"

"I guess so." I looked out the window as trees and houses whizzed past in a blur. All I wanted was to be left alone. The shower of angry words confused me. I couldn't think, yet I *had* to think, to try and figure out what had happened and why.

I didn't understand it. I didn't understand any of it, not the way Jim had made me feel, not the way he ignored me afterward, and not the way I was feeling now: numb, empty, like something had shriveled up inside me.

"How come you didn't scream?"

"What?"

"When he attacked you, how come you didn't scream for help?"

"It happened so fast," I said. "You were there already."

That was the truth. What would have happened if he *hadn't* been there? If he and Jim's father hadn't come out of the house just when they did? I leaned my head against the window. No matter what I tried to imagine happening, it didn't include Jim leaving me under the tree like he'd throw away an empty Coke bottle.

"You didn't encourage him? You must have encouraged him, Venida. Must have given him some idea—"

"I didn't do anything!" I yelled. I twisted around in the seat to look at him. "All I did was get out of the car to stretch my legs. And stop calling me Venida. It's not my name, and I hate it. I hate the way it sounds when you say it! And you have no right to talk to me like this. You're not my father, even though you're pretending to be. What do you care what I do? What do you care what happens to me? Why should you? Nobody else does!"

I slumped back in the seat, feeling the tears starting up in my eyes. Walter must have been pretty shocked by my screaming like that because he didn't say anything for a long time.

"Maybe nobody else cares what happens to you," he said slowly, "but I do. And maybe I haven't got any right to tell you what to do, but I can't help it. You— you get to me, Ven—I mean—oh, hell, what am I supposed to call you anyway? You want me to call you Lauri? Or you want to change it again? Mary, Penelope, Edith—I'll call you any damn name you please."

I reached into my pocketbook and pulled a Kleenex out of my little purse pack. I wiped my eyes with it.

"What do you mean, I get to you? And why should you care about me? You don't even know me."

"And you don't know me. So you don't know what I care about and don't care about."

Walter reached over and flipped the radio on. Twangy banjo music blared out, so loud that you'd have to shout to talk over it. But Walter didn't talk. He just kept his hands tight around the steering wheel and didn't say another word.

We turned onto a main road with two lanes in each direction. It was flatter here, not so hilly, and I began to see billboards on the side of the road. The car picked up speed. We passed a sign that said HOXEY—10 MI.

I watched the billboards whiz by. The Marlboro Man, with his tattoo; a package of Gillette Blue Blades with LOOK SHARP! FEEL SHARP! BE SHARP! in big, black letters; a little boy in pajamas holding a candle and yawning, IT'S TIME TO RE-TIRE. There was a picture of a tire next to him, so I figured they were selling tires, but I didn't know what the boy in pajamas had to do with that.

Now that Walter wasn't yelling at me anymore, I could think. Only now that Walter *had* yelled, I found myself wondering as much about what was going on in Walter's mind as what had been going on in Jim's.

Hoxey turned out to be a fair-sized town, a lot bigger than Winota. It had a real main street, with a drugstore, a five and ten, and a movie theater. *Love Me or Leave Me* was playing. I'd seen it already, but I wouldn't have minded seeing it again. It's a really good movie. Doris Day plays a singer, but it's a very dramatic role and she surprised a lot of people by being such a good actress. James Cagney plays a gangster who loves her, but she doesn't love him, even though he helps her get started with her career, and she becomes famous.

Walter parked the car in front of the Blue Grass Grill.

"We'll eat here," he said. He came around and opened

the door for me. I got out of the car and a couple of boys standing in front of the drugstore looked me over. One of them sort of jabbed the other with his elbow and said something I couldn't hear. The other one grinned and nodded.

Walter took me by the arm and practically pushed me into the Blue Grass Grill.

It was a bar, really, not a restaurant, and pretty dark inside. There were two men sitting at the bar, drinking, and listening to the news on a radio near the cash register.

Walter led me over to a table against the wall and then went to talk to the bartender. Without even asking me what I wanted he ordered two hamburgers and two bourbons.

He came back to the table and sat down opposite me.

"I don't drink," I said.

"They're for me."

I had to go to the bathroom. The bartender pointed toward where it was. I felt like Walter's eyes were stabbing through my back as I walked past the bar to the rest room. It was just a tiny little closet, practically, with a john and a sink, but it was clean.

I used the john and patted cold water on my face. I put on fresh lipstick and pressed powder and checked my hair. It was in a ponytail because I hadn't wanted to take the trouble making a French twist this morning. I smoothed the angel wings in place.

I did all this automatically, without thinking about anything. I felt like I was sleepwalking. It was like I had no control over what was happening to me, and had just about stopped caring or feeling. I was a robot, like in a science-fiction movie, and Walter and Jim and Ruby Durban pushed buttons and made me do things.

When I got back to the table, Walter had one empty glass in front of him and was starting on his second drink.

The bartender brought our hamburgers to the table. I just looked at mine, like I didn't remember what I was supposed to do with a hamburger, or why it was even sitting there in the first place.

"You better eat," Walter said. He picked up his hamburger and took big bites of it. I thought of a lion tearing away at a hunk of raw meat.

They were telling about President Eisenhower on the news, about how his operation was supposed to have been a success, but nobody was sure whether he would run for President again now.

Walter had gotten a Coke for me, which I thought was considerate. I hadn't heard him order it.

I picked up my hamburger and ate it. I don't think I even tasted it. I just bit and chewed and swallowed.

When I was finished, Walter paid the bartender and we went outside. It seemed very bright after the dim light in the bar.

The boys in front of the drugstore were gone.

I looked over at the movie theater. It was called the Palace. There were big posters for *Love Me or Leave Me* on both sides of the ticket booth.

"You going to do any more selling, Walter?" I asked. "Around here, I mean?"

"That's my job."

"Well, how about if I go to that movie over there while you're selling? Then you won't have to explain me or anything, and I—"

"That's very considerate of you, Venida," he said sarcastically. "Worrying about my having to explain you. Well, you just let me do the worrying about that. Come on, I have to get something in here."

He held the drugstore door open for me. I went inside.

There was a big magazine rack in one corner. I went over to look at it while Walter got something from the counter right near the cash register.

The new *Photoplay* was out, with the first pictures of Grace Kelly's wedding to Prince Rainier. I pulled it out of the rack and flipped to the story eagerly. "*A fairy-tale wedding . . .*" it said.

"You want some magazines?" I nearly jumped. Walter was right at my shoulder.

"I know how bored you get just being with me and no TV to watch." His voice was real low, but I could tell he was still being sarcastic. I pretended not to notice.

"If it's all right," I said. I really had to have that magazine.

"Sure. Get whatever you want."

I didn't want to spend too much of his money, even though I was going to pay him back, so I just got the *Photoplay* and a *Silver Screen*. Walter paid for them and we went back to the car.

Walter had a package of Sen-Sen in his hand and was popping the little black squares into his mouth two at a time.

We got into the car and drove down Main Street and turned left. A couple of blocks past Main Street we turned onto a block with big, old houses and really tall trees lining the sidewalk. I looked down the street and there were more houses, as far as I could see. And this was only one street.

I sat back in the seat and sighed. It was going to be a long afternoon.

Walter pulled up in front of the first house on the corner.

"I'll wait for you out here," I said, as he came around to open the door for me. "I can read my magazines."

"Fat chance." He yanked the car door open and waited for me to get out. I just sat there and stared at him.

"What do you mean? Why can't I sit in the car?"

"All alone? A pretty girl like you? You might get *attacked* again. Don't want to take any chances on *that* happening, do we?"

He looked me straight in the eye. His face was angry as a thundercloud. And then, all of a sudden, like I wasn't a robot with no mind anymore, I understood it all.

Walter was jealous.

I know Walter sold a lot of Bibles that afternoon, even though I wasn't paying attention to what was going on in all the houses we called on. But his mood got better and better as those $5 down payments began to fill up his wallet.

I just kept running it all over in my mind. Walter had said he cared about me. He said, "Maybe nobody else cares about you, but I do." And it must have been true. Because it made him jealous to see me with Jim, and why would it make him jealous if he didn't care?

He probably didn't believe that I had nothing to do with what happened under the tree, even though what I told him was the truth. And that made him angry. Here he was driving me to California, and spending money on me, which he probably thought I never planned to pay back, and trying to be pleasant and thoughtful, and the first thing you know, he thinks I'm making out with a perfect stranger.

No wonder he was angry. No wonder he'd been so sarcastic. And hadn't he said, "You get to me"? I didn't realize what he meant when he said it, I was so confused and upset and all, but now I could see he meant he liked me.

Once I had this figured out, I began to wonder what I was supposed to do about it. As I sat there in kitchens and living rooms all afternoon, not listening to Walter sell Bibles, I tried to decide whether it made any difference about anything that Walter liked me.

It was better than not liking me, I guessed, since if he didn't like me he certainly wouldn't drive me to California. But knowing that he liked me, was I supposed to like him?

I remembered how I felt when Jim had been just about to kiss me, then remembered the way I froze up last night when Walter put his lips against my cheek. I looked over at Walter a couple of times during the afternoon, once when he was drinking a cup of coffee a woman had given him. I watched his Adam's apple move as he puckered his lips to blow on the coffee. I tried to imagine those lips on mine, tried to picture how I would feel if Walter took me in his arms and pressed himself against me like Jim had.

But I couldn't imagine it. Once I started trying, all I could think of was Jim, his big, blond head with the hair falling into his eyes, his big, red hands next to my head, his breath on my face.

Was it just that Jim was so tall and handsome, while Walter was old enough to be my father and had a big Adam's apple and a bow tie and wore his belt so high that his pants were practically hitched halfway up his chest?

I didn't know. And I started getting confused again. Maybe the only thing that would un-confuse me was to start concentrating on my movie career, which I hadn't thought about for what seemed to be a very long time. I'd been so distracted by thoughts of Jim and Walter and selling Bibles and poor raggedy children with no shoes, I was forgetting why I was on this trip in the first place.

It was about seven o'clock when we drove up to the Abe Lincoln Inn a few miles outside of Hoxey. It was built like a log cabin and I guess was supposed to look like the house Lincoln was bom in, except for the neon sign on the roof. It was still light out, but the sign was turned on, and flashing red and blue.

Inside, the lights were dim and there were little tables with paper placemats on them. Walter ordered a hamburger for me. He wanted me to get something more expensive, like a steak or something, but I told him I wasn't that hungry. Which I wasn't. He was in a really good mood now, all smiling and talking about how well the selling had gone, and how friendly and hospitable the people of Hoxey were.

I was glad he was in a good mood again, but I would just as soon he kept quiet, so I could fix my mind on my career and what I was going to do when I got to Hollywood. I figured if I just concentrated on my goal, my career, on what I had planned on doing for so long, I could keep a clear head.

I looked down at the paper placemat. It was very interesting. It had a big drawing of Lincoln on it and a whole bunch of puzzles and quizzes and things about Lincoln, plus some little-known facts. I don't really remember any of them.

"We're two of a kind, honey." Walter was leaning over the table, talking in a very low voice. "Two lost souls on the highway of life. One with no ship and one with no rudder."

That sounded familiar. "I think that's a song." I scratched at Lincoln's beard with my fingernail.

"Sure it's a song. It's our song. It could have been written about us. You need a ship and I need a rudder."

I didn't know what he was talking about. He was drinking bourbon and had ordered a New York-cut steak. I wondered about a Bible salesman drinking as much as Walter did. I was also kind of surprised that you had to go clear to Kentucky to get a New York-cut steak. I'd never heard of a New York steak when I was in New York.

"See how it is, honey, you have no ship and I have no rudder. That's why we're two of a kind."

I still didn't get it. I was tired. *Exhausted.* Until the waitress set our food in front of us, I didn't realize how tired I was.

No wonder I couldn't think straight. I felt like all the blood was drained out of my arms and legs, and I suddenly wanted to flop my head right down on the table and go to sleep. My insides actually *sagged.* We'd been driving since eight in the morning . . . it was forever since I'd slept.

I pushed my hamburger away and closed my eyes.

"What is it, honey? You okay?"

"Tired. So tired."

" 'Course you are. I should have realized you're not used to this kind of traveling around. Eat your hamburger, honey.

You must be starving. Long day. You don't even know how hungry you are."

He stabbed a piece of meat with his fork and held it out toward me. "This steak is like butter. Want to try a bite? You can still change your mind and get the steak if you want."

"No, no, that's okay. I'll eat the hamburger."

Walter had two more drinks before we left the restaurant.

"We'd better call it a day," he said as he started up the car. "You really look beat."

"Yes." I leaned back and took a deep breath. It was just getting dark, but it felt like midnight, I was so sleepy.

"There's a nice place a few miles down the road," Walter said. "One of the other salesmen told me about it. Probably no TV, though." He said it teasingly, not like he had before.

"Doesn't matter. All I want to do is go to bed."

"Well, it won't be long now." Walter began to whistle.

In a few minutes he passed a sign that said YOU ARE NOW LEAVING HOXEY! COME BACK SOON! and a little while after that he pulled up in front of the Blue Grass Motel. There were quite a few cars there already, parked in front of room doors, but the VACANCY sign was lit up.

"Be right back," Walter said, and went into the office.

He came back with a key and said, "Number seven. A lucky room."

I just nodded and smiled. He eased the car into the space in front of number seven and came around to help me out. He got my hatbox and his suitcase out of the trunk and I followed him to the room.

He flipped the light switch on and put our bags down near the door. He was whistling again. He closed the door behind us. I heard a little click as the lock snapped.

"Cozy, isn't it?" he said.

"It sure is," I said sleepily. Then I realized how cozy it really was.

"Walter," I said, "there's only one bed."

He was standing right behind me. He wrapped my ponytail around his hand and bent down to whisper in my ear.

"That's all right, honey. It's a nice, *big* bed."

Chapter 12

Maybe I was kidding myself about Walter because I needed him, but after last night, when he hadn't tried anything, I was ready to believe that he was just what he said he was— a kindhearted Bible salesman who liked and respected me and only wanted to help me out. Even today when he got angry, I knew he was only angry because he liked me and cared about me.

But now, here in the Blue Grass Motel, with one bed and Walter's fingers twisted in my hair, I couldn't kid myself anymore. My whole body began to shake.

He put his hands on my shoulders and turned me around to face him. "You are the prettiest thing I ever saw." His voice was thick and I could smell bourbon as he bent his head. I realized he was going to kiss me and I started to back away, but he grabbed my arms before I could escape. I twisted my head around, tried to pull my arms free, but his fingers were like steel in my flesh. His mouth came down on mine and I felt like I was drowning.

I pushed at his chest, hitting out at him, gasping for breath, trying to get away from his mouth. He finally let go of me and I staggered backward. I wiped at my lips, trying to get the taste of Walter's mouth off them. For a minute he just stood there, his eyes fixed on mine like he was hypnotizing me. And for a minute I just stood there, frozen, like he *had* hypnotized me.

"Come on, honey," he said. He was panting for breath,

like he'd just run a race. "You know the score. Don't play hard to get."

He moved toward me and I finally realized I'd better not just stand there like a statue. I made a run for the door, but I hardly had hold of the knob when he grabbed me around the waist from behind and pulled me off my feet.

"No!" I screamed, kicking and struggling. His arms were tight around my stomach. I went crazy with fear and started crying. "Put me down! Put me down! *Don't!*" I kicked backward and felt my heel hit his leg.

"Jesus." He let go of me and I fell onto the floor. I huddled there in a little ball, crying like a baby.

"What is the *matter* with you?" His voice sounded like the hiss of a snake. He bent over me and tried to pull me up by my arm. "What are you crying for?" I shook his hand away and turned my face so he couldn't see it

"Leave me alone. Just leave me alone. What kind of a girl do you think I am?"

"Are you kidding? I know what kind of a girl you are. You hop in a car with a man you've never seen before, you're ready for a little roll in the hay with some shit-kicker you've known for two minutes—"

"You're disgusting! You're drunk and you're disgusting!" I pulled myself up off the floor and stared at him through the tears in my eyes.

"Oh, no," he said. "This isn't the liquor talking. This is me, Walter Murchison, telling you the truth about yourself. You can stop playing your little games. They won't work anymore."

"You're just like all the rest," I said. I felt like I was going to start crying again. I gulped hard, trying to keep the tears from coming. "I thought you were different, but you're not."

"What a coincidence," he said, sarcastic again. "I thought the same thing about you."

"I don't care what you thought about me and I don't care what you think about me now. You can just let me out of here and I'll take care of myself without any help from you. I've been doing it all my life anyway."

"Where are you going to go?" he asked. "It's miles back to Hoxey and you won't have any money when you get there. It's miles to anyplace from here."

And then I couldn't hold it in anymore. I started crying again, not knowing what I could do, except that I *couldn't* take care of myself, I was helpless. I cried louder and louder, feeling such anger at everybody and everything that I couldn't do anything but scream it out.

I flew at Walter, and began hitting his shoulders with my fists. There were so many other people I wanted to hit, a whole string of them, starting with my mother, who loved drinking more than she loved me, right up through Uncle Ted. Walter was just the last person in the string, the newest disappointment, and he was *here.*

"Hey, hey, take it easy. Stop yelling, will you?" He grabbed my wrists to keep me from hitting him. "What are you doing that for? Hey, stop it, pipe down. Please, Venida, stop yelling, I'm sorry, I—"

"My name isn't Venida! It's *Sylvie, Sylvie, Sylvie!*"

And then, all of a sudden, he was holding me in his arms and I was crying against his shirt, but not loudly now, just like a little child who couldn't stop.

He patted me on the back gently. "Sylvie," he said. He

said it again, like he was tasting it, rolling it around on his tongue. "Sylvie. Like the song. Why would you want to change that? Such a pretty name. And unusual. Not like Sylvia." His voice was soft and soothing.

The sound of his voice and the feel of his arms around me, gentle now, like a father's, made me calmer and in a few minutes I wasn't crying anymore, just leaning against him, trying to catch my breath.

"I'm sorry if I misjudged you, Sylvie. I just never met anyone like you before. And I couldn't help it. I wasn't kidding when I said you get to me. You do. I felt it the first minute I laid eyes on you in that restaurant. Why do you think I offered to drive you clear to California?"

I pulled away from him and frowned. "What are you talking about?"

"Love, Sylvie. I'm talking about love!"

"You're crazy," I whispered. I shook my head. I felt dizzy. "You just met me yesterday. How could you love me?"

"I'm not crazy. I'd be crazy to drive you across the country if I *didn't* love you. *That* would be crazy. Why do you think I was so angry about seeing you with that kid?"

"But you said you were just driving me because—"

"I know what I said. I had to say something, didn't I? You don't believe me now, so what would you have thought if I told you I loved you ten seconds after we met?"

Love.

Love. The word kept repeating in my head like an echo, except, instead of getting softer and fading away, it seemed to get louder and louder, like someone was shouting it inside my brain.

I sort of flopped down into the chair near the door, trying to understand what was happening.

Walter loved me. He said so. Nobody ever loved me in my whole life, let alone told me they did. I don't even think my grandmother loved me. I think she just took me in because she had to, because she was the only relative I had.

But this was crazy. Love at first sight only happens in the movies. You can learn a lot from the movies, but I know perfectly well that real life doesn't usually work out like it does in pictures, even though lots of times I wish it would.

Yet, even in the car when he was angry after seeing me with Jim, Walter had said he cared about me. He cared what I did. Why would he care if he didn't love me? That was just as crazy as loving me. If he didn't love me, why should he be angry about Jim?

"You're awful quiet, Sylvie. See, I'm not having any trouble remembering to call you that. I guess Lauri just didn't feel like it was right for you. So, what do you think, Sylvie?"

"About what?" I could hardly think at *all*.

"About what I said. I know you think I'm crazy and maybe I am, but what do you think?"

"I don't know what to think. I'm so confused about everything."

"I meant what I said about the ship and the rudder, too. Remember?"

I just nodded.

"Sylvie, if I don't do any more selling, we can make it to Las Vegas in three days, and still get you to Los Angeles in plenty of time for your screen test."

I didn't know what was going on. Ten minutes ago he was screaming at me, practically calling me a tramp, trying to attack me, and now he was talking about love and ships and rudders and driving to Las Vegas. I was getting more mixed up by the minute.

My head was spinning. The part about not doing any more selling sounded fine to me, and the sooner I got to Los Angeles the better, but should I get there with Walter? After what happened tonight, how could I be sure he wouldn't try it again? Maybe he really *was* crazy. But maybe he really did love me, and that explained everything. Maybe *I'm* crazy, I thought.

And why Las Vegas? What did Walter want to stop there for, unless he was a gambler?

"Why not just go straight to Los Angeles, Walter?" I asked. "Why do we have to stop at Las Vegas?"

"Because there's no waiting period there."

"What? What does that mean, no waiting period?"

Walter laughed. "It means we don't have to wait."

"Wait for what?"

"To get married."

Chapter 13

Dear Mom,

The craziest thing has happened. On my way to California my wallet got stolen on the bus and I met a man who's driving me there and asked me to marry him.

I don't know what to do. This is one of those times I wish you were here so I could talk to you and you could give me advice. I never told you this, but one of the reasons I want to make it in the movies is I have this dream. I guess it sounds kind of babyish, but ever since I decided to be a movie star, I've been dreaming it. One day you'll see me in a movie and recognize me even though you haven't seen me in so long, and you'll say, "That's my daughter!" and come to Hollywood to find me. And I'll be making plenty of money and be able to take care of you and we can live together for the rest of our lives.

I guess it does sound silly. I don't even know if they have movies where you are. . . .

I never actually told Walter I would marry him. But I never actually told Walter I wouldn't marry him, either. I guess I sort of let him think I wanted to go to Las Vegas and "tie the knot" as fast as possible, because we were out of the Blue Grass Motel and back on the road before I knew what was happening.

Walter seemed really eager to get married.

And I was really eager to get out of that motel.

I was so exhausted I slept in the back seat of the car the rest of the night.

The next three days are practically as blurry in my mind as the view from Walter's car window was. He drove like he was trying to set speed records. The only time he slowed down was to read the Burma Shave signs.

They were really cute. I never saw them before, but Walter said they were all over the places where he drove. The first batch we came to made me laugh, so after that Walter slowed down every time he saw them coming up, so I could read them out loud.

What they were, were little signs by the side of the road. You'd see one first and it would have one line of a poem on it, then a little way down the road there was another sign with the second line of the poem, and you'd read the poem like that, sign by sign, until you got to the last sign, which always said: BURMA SHAVE.

Some of them were really clever. My favorite was:

Dinah doesn't. ..
Treat him right...
But if he'd shave ...
Dyna-mite!
BURMA SHAVE.

Walter did a lot of the driving at night because he said we'd make better time that way. He'd drive till about three in the afternoon, then we'd eat a big meal and he'd fall asleep in a motel room till eight or nine at night, and we'd start out again. He bought me movie magazines to read, because I couldn't go to sleep in the middle of the day like that—and I didn't want to, anyway, in the same room with Walter. I suppose I would have been safe enough, though, because he was so tired from all those hours of driving that he'd fall asleep the minute his head hit the pillow. And he made sure to stop only at motels that had TV, which I thought was very considerate of him.

I slept during the night, curled up on the back seat of the Pontiac, listening to the soft music on the radio, and to Walter humming along with the songs he knew.

I didn't know what I was going to do when we got to Las Vegas.

At first, the only thought in my mind was, At least we're not in the Blue Grass Motel and Walter isn't pawing me anymore.

But somewhere along the way I started thinking about having Walter to take care of me, like he said he wanted. I pictured myself in a little bungalow in California, wearing a frilly apron and preparing Walter's breakfast. I could picture the sun streaming in from the window over the sink, making the kitchen all bright and cheery. I could even see the lemon tree that would grow right next to the house, and almost smell the coffee Walter was drinking.

I read this article about Ginger Rogers and they had pictures of her in her kitchen, wearing a pinafore apron and whipping up dinner and she said that was the most fulfilling part of her life. She said it was even better than being a movie star.

And there was the story about Janet Leigh and Tony Curtis. Janet Leigh said the most important thing in the world to her was to be a good wife and mother, and compared to that being a famous actress was very unimportant.

But Janet Leigh loves Tony Curtis. I didn't love Walter. How could I even think about marrying a man I didn't love?

But Walter loved me. Maybe that was more important. And maybe it was just too soon to know whether I loved Walter or not. I didn't know anything about love. Maybe it takes a while before you realize you love someone.

But it only took Walter ten seconds. Well, maybe it's different for men. Like I said, I didn't know anything about love.

Except that nobody ever said they loved me before.

But, my *career*. I didn't set off on a Greyhound bus to find a husband. I was going to be a movie star.

Well, there was no reason I couldn't be a wife *and* a movie star, which is what I really want anyhow. And I do want children. Two girls. Twins, I hoped, like Honey and Bunny.

Maybe I was too young to get married, but maybe I was also too young to tackle Hollywood all by myself. I had no money, no job, no appointment for a screen test like Walter thought. And my first day on my own I got myself robbed.

Maybe it wasn't such a bad idea to have someone to take care of me while I tried to get into the movies. And if I found out by the time I was a star I didn't love him—well, a divorce isn't the most terrible thing in the world, I guess.

But . . . "When I get married it'll be for *keeps*."

The closer we got to Las Vegas, the harder it got for me to think straight.

I'd find myself looking over at Walter and wondering how I could love James Dean and Harry Belafonte and even think about marrying someone like Walter. And I couldn't very well hang out with the "young crowd" and go on double dates with Natalie if I was married.

And then I'd think, if I don't marry him, what am I going to do? He's going to be pretty upset after I let him drive me all the way to Nevada thinking we were going to be married, and then I back out. He certainly wouldn't smile and say, That's okay, I understand, here's some money, go to California and good luck in the movies. No, I'd be stranded in Nevada.

But maybe I could get a job in Las Vegas and earn the money to get the rest of the way to California on my own. After all, even if I don't know anything about geography, I know Nevada is pretty near California. And a lot of people from California go to Las Vegas for a vacation. I could even hitchhike to California with some of the people on their way back home.

And then, suddenly, there was no more time to think.

Walter was in the back seat with me, shaking me gently. "Wake up, honey, we're here."

I sat up and looked out the window. It felt like it was practically the middle of the night, but the street was filled with people, signs flashed on and off, and at the end of the street there was a huge neon cowboy on top of a building. He was blazing with colored lights and stood looking out over the street as if he was the king of Las Vegas or something.

"Why are there so many people out?" I asked sleepily. "Is there a fire or something?"

Walter laughed. "That's Vegas for you, honey. Nobody sleeps here. They gamble all night long."

"Oh."

Walter put his arm around me and I shivered.

"Gets chilly here at night," he said. He held me tighter. "It'll be plenty hot in the daytime, don't you worry."

"Why are we stopped here?"

Walter pointed out the window. In between two neon signs was a small building with a white door and a regular painted sign hanging on a post. JUSTICE OF THE PEACE, the sign read.

"We're going to get married," Walter said.

"Now?"

"Sure. Why not? That's what we came here for, isn't it?"

"Well, yes, but—" Frantically I tried to think. I'd had three days to think and hadn't been able to come up with any real ideas about what I was going to do. I don't know how I expected to come up with one now.

"But it's the middle of the night!"

"That's the great thing about this town," Walter said happily. "You can get married any time of the day or night. You just walk in and ask to get married, and five minutes later you're man and wife. When they say 'no waiting period' they really mean it!"

"But, Walter!" I cried. "That's not the way I want to get married!"

He let go of me. "What do you mean? How did you think you were going to get married? In a church with a white gown and twelve bridesmaids?"

"No, but—"

"But what, Sylvie? I don't get it."

"Walter, look at me!"

He looked. And his eyes got all soft and dreamy. He

had exactly the same expression on his face that Danny Kaye gets when he meets Virginia Mayo for the first time.

"I'm looking," he said.

"No, I mean it. Look at my clothes, my hair. I'm a *mess*. I don't want to get married like this. What kind of a wedding would that be? I want to look pretty for my wedding, Walter. I want to look pretty for *you*." I don't know how I thought of that. It just popped out, but it must have been the right thing to say.

"I guess a girl dreams about her wedding day all her life," Walter said thoughtfully.

"That's right. And it's something to remember all your life, too. I don't want to remember getting married in dirty, crummy old clothes in the middle of the night like some—some—"

"Okay, okay, Sylvie, I understand. I guess it wouldn't be such a bad idea to wait a few hours. You can get a new dress and I can get some sleep. I'm pretty beat anyhow."

I nearly cried with relief. We got into the front seat of the Pontiac and Walter drove around until he found a motel with a VACANCY sign lit up.

It was called the Lucky Silver Horseshoe Motel, and as Walter opened the door to our room, he said, "Look, Sylvie, it even has TV. Not that we'll be watching much TV... His eyes sort of glittered when he said that, and I felt a little shudder go through me.

All I could see of the room was one big bed.

I looked at that bed and I looked at Walter's glittery eyes and all of a sudden a lot of things got really clear in my head.

Marriage was not just wearing a frilly apron and pouring coffee. If I married Walter I'd have to sleep in that bed with him. How can you do that with somebody you don't love? I'd been trying not to think about that for the past three days, but now I realized that the only reason Walter wanted to marry me was because that was *all* he'd been thinking about for the past three days.

Walter didn't really love me. Maybe he thought he did, and I'm not too sure about that even, but he didn't *really* love me. He just wanted sex and he knew by this time I'm not the kind of girl who'd go all the way without being married. Here in Las Vegas there was no waiting period so he could marry me real fast. He'd been divorced a long time, so he was probably pretty eager to have a wife again.

And maybe he even thought if he got tired of me he could divorce me in Reno. I know a lot of movie stars and famous people get divorced in Reno, which is also in Nevada. Hadn't Walter said his first wife divorced him in Reno? I guess there's no waiting period there either. So it wouldn't be very hard to get rid of me if he found out he didn't really love me after all.

"Come on, honey," Walter said, taking me by the arm. "Let's get some sleep and then we'll buy you the prettiest dress you ever saw."

He tried to lead me over to the bed, but I pulled away. "We're not married yet, Walter," I said. We won't *ever* be married, I thought.

"I know, I know, honey. We'll just sleep. I won't lay a finger on you, I promise. Be reasonable. There's only one bed, and we both need to sleep."

"Not in the same bed," I said firmly. "Not until we're married."

Never. *Never.*

I looked around the room. "I'll sleep on that chair."

"How can you sleep in a chair?" he said impatiently. "You won't be very comfortable."

"If I can sleep in the back seat of a car, I can sleep in a chair."

"All right, have it your own way. It won't be long now anyway."

He took off his jacket and hung it in the closet. He started to undo his belt, then looked over at me. I guess I had a pretty shocked expression on my face, because he sort of shrugged and buckled it up again.

"At least give me a little kiss, Sylvie," he said coaxingly. "After all, we're engaged. There's nothing wrong with kissing your fiancé."

I nodded. I couldn't very well refuse that. He held me by the shoulders and I took a deep breath, like I was getting ready to dive into a swimming pool. I held it while he pressed his lips against mine, gently at first, but then harder and harder until I pulled away when I couldn't hold my breath anymore.

"You better stop, Walter. You don't want to get carried away."

"I'm already carried away," he panted. "I just wish you'd get carried away too. Kiss me again, Sylvie." He pulled me against him and started running his hands down my back. I squirmed out of his arms.

"Walter, if you don't stop I'll walk out of this room right this minute." And I would, too, even if I didn't have the slightest idea where I'd go or what I'd do.

He must have known I meant it because he said, "Sylvie, you are the most—*virtuous* girl I ever ran into." He sounded really annoyed about it.

"You're a Bible salesman, Walter," I reminded him. "Would you marry a girl who wasn't good? And besides, a couple of days ago you didn't think I was—virtuous—at all."

"Well, I misjudged you," he grumbled.

"I think a Bible salesman ought to be virtuous too," I said sternly.

"Will you stop harping on that?" he snapped. "Just because I peddle Bibles doesn't mean I don't have *needs.*"

He lay down on the bed and put his hands behind his head. I turned off the lamp. The sun was just coming up and it was pretty light in the room, so I pulled the window shades down.

I sat back in the orange plastic chair. It wasn't very comfortable. I looked over at Walter on the bed. His eyes were still open and he was staring up at the ceiling. I wished he'd gotten a room with two beds. But why should he? He thought we were getting married in a couple of hours.

I was so tired I wanted to lie down and go to sleep.

I shut my eyes and tried to think. I had to forget about being tired, I had to forget about sleeping. I had to figure out a *plan*. And I only had a few hours left.

Think, I told myself, *think*. You got yourself into this, Sylvie Krail, and no one but you can get you out of it.

And that's the last thing I remember before I fell asleep sitting up in the orange plastic chair.

Chapter 14

When I woke up, Walter was lying under the bedspread, snoring. I jumped out of the chair, wondering what time it was, and how I could have let myself fall asleep like that when I was supposed to be *thinking*.

I peeked out the window, just moving the shade up a little bit; it was bright and sunny. It must be pretty late. Walter would probably wake up any minute.

I had to do *something*. I could just walk out of the Lucky Silver Horseshoe Motel and disappear in the crowds, but then what? I didn't have any money, and even my hatbox was locked in the trunk of Walter's car. I looked over at the night table. There were no keys on it. Walter must still have them in his pocket.

Maybe I could borrow some money from Walter. While he was asleep. He said he'd buy me a dress anyhow, so if I just borrowed as much as he would have spent on the dress . . .

But I couldn't kid myself. That wouldn't be borrowing, that would be stealing. Even if I could get to his wallet without waking him up, I couldn't take his money. No matter what his reasons were, he'd already gone to a lot of trouble and expense for me. It was bad enough that I'd let him think we were going to get married without stealing from him on top of it.

I could tell him the truth. The whole truth. Why I deceived him the way I did, why I had to go to California, why he was my only hope. And then ask him for one more bit of help—just enough money to get to Los Angeles and live on until I got a job.

That would never work. Why would he give me any money? He'd just think I'd lied to him and used him, and he'd be angry that I wasn't going to marry him after all he'd done for me. I'd seen Walter angry in the Blue Grass Motel. I didn't want to see him angry again.

I could give up.

I could go to a police station and tell them who I was and the police would call Aunt Grace and Uncle Ted and they'd come and get me and take me home.

Home. Robin Lane. Aunt Grace. Honey and Bunny. Uncle Ted.

Suddenly I realized I wasn't hearing Walter snoring anymore. I whirled around to look at the bed. He'd turned over onto his side. I stood there, frozen, not even breathing, waiting to see if he was waking up. But he didn't open his eyes and in a moment he was breathing deeply and evenly, his arm wrapped around the pillow like it was . . . like it was *me*.

I grabbed my pocketbook from the dresser and tiptoed to the door. Whatever I was going to do, I knew I couldn't stay here. I turned the doorknob very gently, hoping the door wouldn't creak. I looked back at Walter. Maybe I ought to leave him a note, apologizing, explaining things, thanking him.

But he might wake up any minute. There was no time for a note.

I opened the door just enough to let myself out. It didn't creak. I closed it softly behind me.

And felt like I'd stepped into a furnace. The sun was blazing; I thought it must be a hundred degrees. It was even worse than Arizona, where we'd stopped yesterday. It was worse than *anything*.

I leaned against the room door. I felt a little dizzy. The cars in the parking spaces sort of shimmered and looked wavy in the sunlight. I thought I'd better stand there for a minute until I got used to it.

I took out my pressed powder compact and my lipstick from my pocketbook. From what I could see of myself in the little mirror, I didn't look too bad. I'd just washed my hair yesterday and put it in the French twist again. The angel wings were holding up okay. All my cosmetics were in my hatbox, so I could only put on the pressed powder and lipstick. I didn't think I looked eighteen, even with the French twist.

I wished I had some other clothes to wear. I'd rinsed out my boat-neck top and put on my one other clean blouse yesterday, but I was still wearing the same black capri pants.

How could I find a job looking like this?

I didn't know where to go, but I knew I couldn't just stand there against the door. Any minute Walter might wake up, find I was gone, and open that door to look for me.

I started walking. I didn't know which way to walk, but what difference did it make? I went past the doors to the rooms, past the office, and turned right. There was another motel across the street. It had a giant pair of dice on the roof and the sign read, Lucky 7-11 Motel. I wondered if everything in Las Vegas was named after things to do with gambling.

There weren't nearly as many people around this street

in the middle of the day as there were on that street we'd stopped at before sunrise. I guess there weren't any places around here to gamble. All I saw were motels, a drugstore, a little grocery, and a liquor store.

I crossed the street. The Lucky 7-11 Motel had a pool on the side. There was nobody around except two little kids splashing in the pool and a guy in a turned-down white sailor cap sitting near the diving board.

I think I would have given anything for a bathing suit at that minute. The kids were ducking each other and screaming, and splashing water around, and the sun was beating down on my head and I was almost tempted to jump in that pool with all my clothes on and start splashing with them.

I walked around the side of the pool and stood near where they were playing.

"Hey, you'll get wet!" the guy in the sailor cap called.

"I don't mind," I said. "I hope I do."

"Why don't you put on your suit and hop in?"

"I'm not staying at this motel," I said.

He looked around, as if someone might be watching, then pulled himself up and walked toward me. He was all tan and muscley, with dark, dark hair on his chest and legs. He was about the same height as Walter, but when he got up close I could see he was much younger. And much better looking, too. I sort of stared at him.

And he stared back.

"Listen," he said softly, "they don't care who uses the pool. It doesn't matter if you're not staying here."

I wondered why he was whispering if they didn't care, but all I said was, "I don't have a bathing suit anyway."

He looked me up and down and I got embarrassed and

annoyed, like I always do when that happens.

"Just as well," he said finally. "You're so light you'd burn in five minutes."

"I wish you'd stop looking at me like that." I turned a little away from him and pretended to watch the kids in the pool.

"I'll bet you're used to it."

I turned back to him. "That doesn't mean I like it."

He smiled, a sort of apologetic little grin. "No, I guess not. Sorry. I've never seen you around here before."

"We just got here last night. This morning, really."

A blond woman came out of one of the doors of the motel calling, "Johnnie! Barbara! Come on out of there now." The kids yelled, "No! No!" and ducked under the water.

"I hope they weren't too much trouble, Vic," the woman called.

"No trouble at all."

Vic, that was his name. I guessed he was supposed to be watching the kids. Was he a baby-sitter or something?

"Johnnie! Get out of that pool this minute!" the woman yelled. "Barbara, I *mean* it. Come on, now, I have a surprise for you."

"I'll get them out, Mrs. Benson," Vic said. He jumped into the pool right next to the kids and made a big roaring sound. They screamed and giggled and tried to splash water in his eyes.

"The giant whale is coming to get you!" he roared. "The giant whale is coming to get you!" They jumped up and down, shrieking with laughter, and he grabbed them around the waist, one in each arm.

"The giant whale got you! The giant whale is throwing you back on shore!" He leaned over the edge of the pool and put them both down gently on the tile next to the rim.

Their mother grabbed them before they could jump back in.

"Thanks, Vic." She pulled the kids into their room and slammed the door.

I was laughing as Vic got out of the water.

"My whale imitation," he said, shaking the water off. "It slays the audience. Come on, you better get in the shade."

We walked over to a table with a big green umbrella over it. We sat down on two green iron chairs. It wasn't really any cooler under the umbrella, but at least the sun was out of my eyes.

"Are you their baby-sitter?" I asked.

"More like their keeper," he laughed. "No, not really. I'm the pool attendant here. I keep the pool clean, take care of things, make sure nobody drowns, all that jazz."

"That sounds like an interesting job." It didn't really, but I didn't know what else to say, and I wanted to keep talking to this boy.

He was a boy, I realized, but not young. I thought he must be about nineteen or twenty. I was sure he wasn't in high school. He was much more mature than any of the boys I knew.

"It's not my life's work," he said. "Just a summer job. And the tips are pretty good—at least when people are winning. Who's 'we'?"

"What?" I didn't know what he meant.

"You were telling me, 'We just got here last night.' Who's 'we'?"

"Oh. Walter and me."

"Who's Walter? For that matter, who are you? No, tell me who Walter is first."

"It's a long story." I looked out at the pool.

"There's no one in there," he said. "I have plenty of time to listen."

"Tell me about yourself first," I said. I felt very shy and self-conscious. And I felt something else, too. I felt like I did when I wanted Jim to kiss me under that tree in Kentucky. I wondered again if a person can tell when you feel that way? Jim must have been able to, because he was going to kiss me before we were interrupted. Could Vic tell too? I began to be really embarrassed. I stared down at my lap, afraid to look him in the eye.

"Won't you even tell me your name?" he asked. "No, let me guess. I'll bet I can guess it."

"No you couldn't," I mumbled.

"I have amazing psychic powers," Vic said, in a spooky sort of voice. "I see all, know all."

I looked up, startled. Could he really read my mind? Did he know what I was thinking about him?

He got this funny look on his face for a second and frowned a little, but then began talking in that phony spooky voice real fast.

"Of course, it's coming, it's coming. Your name is . . . Esmeralda."

I giggled. "It is not."

"All right, all right, no, don't tell me, I've got it. .. Euphronia."

"No!"

"I don't understand it. My psychic powers have never

failed me before. Let me concentrate. . . ."

I was giggling so hard now I must have sounded like one of those little kids in the pool, but I couldn't stop myself. I didn't *want* to stop myself. I don't know why, but it was fun to feel like a six-year-old.

"I know it begins with an E . . . Ernestine!"

"No! And it doesn't begin with an E."

"I don't suppose it's Rumpelstiltskin?"

I was laughing so hard now all I could do was shake my head.

"It's—it's Sylvie," I finally gasped.

He turned his mouth down. "Oh," he said, sounding disappointed. "I liked Euphronia so much better."

I wiped at my eyes with my hands. I'd laughed so hard I was practically crying.

Then Vic leaned over and said, suddenly, "Sylvie, who's Walter?"

Before I even had time to think I blurted out, "He wants to marry me."

I was surprised I said it. I didn't mean to tell Vic about that. I never should have mentioned Walter in the first place. I don't know why I did.

But if I was surprised, Vic was stunned.

"*Marry* you? How the hell old are you?"

"Eighteen," I said haughtily.

"Sylvie, I've been eighteen. You're not eighteen."

"Well, going on eighteen. Practically—"

"I've been seventeen too. And sixteen and fifteen and fourteen—"

"I'm not fourteen!" I cried.

He sat back in the chair and looked at me like he was

sort of studying my face. I realized that when I said I wasn't fourteen, I'd just about admitted what my real age was. But suddenly I felt I didn't have to pretend with Vic. I didn't want to pretend; I was tired of pretending.

"Does he know you're only fifteen?"

"No. He thinks I'm going on nineteen."

"You're kidding."

"I look a lot older with makeup!" I said indignantly.

"I'll bet. How old is he?"

"I don't know exactly. I'm not sure."

"You don't *know?*"

"I guess in his thirties. Maybe thirty-five."

"Why do you want to marry a thirty-five-year-old man? A *maybe thirty-five-year-old* man?"

"Well, I don't, not anymore. I mean, I don't think I ever *really* wanted to marry him. I just didn't know what else to do."

"You could finish high school."

I sighed. "I told you this was a long story."

"And I told you I had plenty of time. The pool is clean, the guests are busy at the slot machines; my boss is making sure the maid isn't stealing the towels. Go on. Tell me about Walter."

So I did.

From the time I got on the Greyhound bus in New York, until this morning, I told Vic everything that happened to me. My wallet being stolen or lost, meeting Walter, selling Bibles, even about Jim. It was so easy talking to Vic, even though I'd never seen him before in my life. Maybe that's why it was so easy.

I didn't tell him about anything that happened before

I got on the bus. I just told him I was going to Hollywood to be an actress.

He listened to the whole thing without saying a word, though his eyes seemed to get really dark and angry when I told him about the night in the Blue Grass Motel.

When I was finally finished I gave sort of a weak little laugh and said, "It sounds kind of crazy, doesn't it?"

Vic took a deep breath and nodded. "Oh, yeah. Crazy. Why were you running away from home?"

"I wasn't running away," I said nervously. "I was running *to*. To Hollywood. To be in the movies."

"You had a home in New York?"

"Sort of."

"What do you mean, sort of? Did you live in a house? Did you have parents? Are you an orphan who just walked the streets for fifteen years and then hopped on a bus for Hollywood?"

That's when I burst into tears. I don't know why, except maybe the word *orphan* set me off, but there I was, sobbing like I had a "Cry" switch and someone had just pulled it.

Vic jumped out of his chair. "Hey, I'm sorry, I didn't mean—"

He put his arm around my shoulder. "Look, you must be exhausted. Come on, I know a place you can rest. It's air-conditioned and everything."

I stumbled from the chair and followed him to the end of the row of doors. He opened one and pulled me inside. It was hot and stuffy, but he flipped a switch and I heard an air conditioner start up.

"It'll be cool in a little while," he said. "I'm sorry there aren't any sheets on the bed, but they never make this room up. The mattress is clean though, and on my lunch hour maybe I can sneak you in some linens."

"What if somebody comes?"

"Nobody'll come. They don't use this room. The bathroom tile is all coming off and they have to put a whole new wall in there. Everything works, it just looks lousy. Why don't you lie down and try and get some sleep. I'll be back on my lunch hour—in about an hour and a half. I'll bring you something to eat and some Cokes and we'll talk about what to do, okay?"

"Oh, Vic." He was so *good*. Before I realized what I was doing, I had my arms around his neck and was pulling his head down so I could kiss him. I held onto him for dear life, pressing my lips against his so hard I could feel his teeth against my mouth. I don't know what got into me, I just knew I had to hold him, had to feel him holding me, kissing me, loving me, and if I let go of him, I was afraid I would die.

For a moment he put his arms around me. For a moment he pressed me against himself and kissed me back. But then he reached up and pulled my arms away from his neck.

"Jesus," he muttered. "Sylvie, you shouldn't."

He stepped back. He looked sort of shaky, and he had the strangest look in his eyes, almost like he was frightened or something.

"I'm sorry!" I wailed. "Vic, I'm sorry, I didn't mean—"

"Shh. Shh." He held his finger up to his lips, then sort of felt around them, like I had injured him or something.

I was so ashamed I wanted to hide.

"We have to keep our voices down," he said.

"I'm sorry," I whispered miserably. "I'm really sorry. That was terrible, I—"

"No it wasn't. It was very nice. You just—surprised me a little."

"It *was* terrible." I began to cry again. "You must think I'm a tramp. I've known you for ten minutes—"

"An hour," he interrupted, "and I really hate that word. You want to know what I think of you? I think you're tired and scared and alone and I don't blame you one bit. Well, there's nothing to be scared of here, and you're not alone anymore, and if you'll just lie down on that bed and sleep until I get back you won't be tired either."

I sat down on the bed. I was still crying, but not so hard.

Vic wiped my tears away with his fingers. I clutched at his hand, holding his knuckles against my cheek.

"I won't leave you, Sylvie," he said softly. "I'll be back at one o'clock, I promise. I won't leave you alone."

I nodded and let go of his hand. He stood there for a minute, then bent down and kissed me very gently on the forehead.

"I have to get back to work now. Lie down. Get some sleep. And stay in this room, okay? Don't go out. We don't want anyone to know you're here. Okay, Sylvie?"

"Okay."

He peeked out the window and then let himself out of the room.

I curled up on the bed, holding the black-and-white-striped pillow against me like it was—

Like it was Vic.

Chapter 15

I was asleep when Vic came back. I woke up to find him sitting in a chair across from the bed, looking at me.

I sat up, confused and somehow sort of embarrassed. I don't know why. I'd practically thrown myself at him, so I don't understand why I should be embarrassed to have him watch me sleeping, but I was.

"How long have you been here?"

"Just a couple of minutes. I brought you a deluxe lunch."

"Thank you. I'll pay you back."

"You will not. You don't owe me anything. And you *won't* owe me anything. Know what I mean?"

"No."

"Never mind. Eat this deluxe lunch."

"Gee, I'm hungry. What is it?"

He opened a bag on the dresser and took out a whole bunch of stuff. He'd gotten roast beef sandwiches, chicken salad sandwiches, cole slaw, potato salad, pickles, potato chips, Cokes, and two big pieces of angel food cake.

"Oh, Vic, this is fabulous!" Nothing had ever tasted so good. Nothing, ever. All I could do was eat. And eat. And eat.

"Do you always pick at your food like this?" he asked.

I giggled, but my mouth was full, so I tried to giggle with my mouth closed. I shook my head no.

"Well," he said, between bites of his sandwich, "I know you're dying to hear the story of my life."

I nodded hard.

"I knew you were. My name is Victor Firenze. I'm twenty years old. I'm in my third year at UCLA. I'm taking a premed course. I want to be a psychiatrist when I grow up."

"That's really interesting," I said. "Do you know, a lot of movie stars go to psychiatrists? Some of them go *five times a week!*"

"You see, it isn't all tinsel and glamour."

"I know that." I looked at him and realized he was trying very hard not to laugh. "You're teasing me," I said.

"A little. Do you mind?"

"No. I think I like it. See, the thing is, I really don't know how to talk to boys."

"You're doing fine. Anyone would think you'd been talking to boys your entire life. Well, as I was saying, some day, after many years of struggle, I'm going to be a psychiatrist. I have a mother and a father, and a sister a year older than you. Which means I'm old enough to be your brother."

I laughed again. I was finishing off the angel food cake and feeling around in the bag for stray potato chips.

"Now tell me about your family."

I stopped laughing.

"I haven't got any. Not really."

"You *are* an orphan?"

"No, not exactly. I have a mother. But she's—"

I crumpled up the potato chip bag. "This is another long story," I said angrily.

"I'd like to hear it."

I squeezed and squeezed the bunched-up bag between my fingers. "I don't know if I can tell it without starting to cry again."

"That's okay," Vic said. "I don't mind."

"Well, I do. Lately all I do is cry and feel sorry for myself. You'd think I'd be cried out by this time."

"Nobody's ever cried out, Sylvie."

"Maybe not...."

I told him everything. Everything I had never told anyone else before, I told Vic. About Mr. Framer, Mr. O'Connor, Uncle Ted—all the secrets I'd been hiding from everyone, all the things that made me ashamed, all the reasons why I had to get on that Greyhound bus. Except for one.

And I kept my voice very firm and swallowed every time I thought I might cry, so I made it through the whole thing without one tear coming out.

When I was finished, he just sat there for a few minutes, his arms folded, sort of staring off into space.

I wondered what he was thinking. I wondered what he thought about me, now that he'd heard everything.

Suddenly I found I was shivering, and it wasn't because the air conditioner was on.

It was kind of a relief to finally have somebody to tell it all to, but it was also a little scary. I crossed my arms over my chest and held onto myself, trying to stop the shaking.

I heard noises from the pool. Vic looked at his watch. "I'm going to have to get back to work in a few minutes. Come here, Sylvie."

I got up and walked toward him, my legs all wobbly. He pulled me onto his lap and wrapped his arms around me, tight, tighter, till I *did* start to cry. I buried my face in his shoulder, getting his neck all wet with my tears. But he didn't mind and neither did I, because as the tears came out the shivering began to stop. I started to get the strangest feeling of—I don't know what to call it—it was like I was released from something. Like I'd been chained up for years, and these tears were finally washing away the chains. I know it doesn't make any sense, but that's the way I felt.

But there was just one thing. One more piece of the chain. I knew I had to tell Vic now, no matter what he thought of me, or I'd still have that piece of chain with me for the rest of my life.

Maybe that's why I'd been shivering so hard. Maybe I knew I had to tell him, and was afraid. I'd stopped shaking, but I was still afraid.

"Vic?" I kept my face against his shoulder. I didn't want to look at him, didn't want him to look at me.

"Yes?"

"There's one more thing. It's really bad, Vic. It's terrible. But I have to tell you. You'll think I'm awful and I don't want you to think I'm awful."

"I won't think you're awful."

"Do you promise? *Promise*, Vic."

"I promise. No matter what."

"You know what I was telling you about—about Uncle Ted? And what he was trying—I mean, how he always—"

"Yes?"

"Well, that wasn't the only reason I had to get out."

"What's the other reason?" Vic asked gently.

"I—I was afraid."

"Afraid of what?"

"Of—of—I can't say it!"

"Yes you can. Say it, Sylvie."

"Of myself. I was afraid—I'd let him. *I wanted him to.*"

Chapter 16

"I don't think that's so unusual," Vic said.

I was so stunned at the matter-of-fact way he said it, I jumped off his lap and almost shouted.

"Didn't you hear what I said?"

"Shh! Keep your voice down. Yes, I heard what you said."

"But it's terrible! How can you be so—so—"

"Listen, I just promised I wouldn't think it was terrible, didn't I? Now you're mad at me because I'm keeping my promise. Well, I'm sorry if you're mad, but it's not terrible. It's natural."

"Natural? Are you crazy? How can it be natural? How could I feel that way? Don't you understand, that makes me a—"

"Sylvie, I swear I'll bash you one if you use that word again. Now calm down and listen to me a minute. I've got to get back to the pool. I hate to leave you like this, but I can't help it I'll be back at four-thirty. I get off at four, but I want to run home and change."

"Vic!"

"Look, you can figure it out. Think about what every kid needs."

"I know what every kid needs," I said irritably. "I don't have to think about that. Love."

"Very good. You have the makings of a fine psychiatrist."

"I don't want to be a psychiatrist. I want to be an actress." I was really getting exasperated with Vic. And confused. He wasn't reacting at all like I expected and I didn't know what to make of it.

"Okay. Then why do you *really* want to be one?"

He pushed back the window shade an inch. "I don't know why I'm looking to see if anyone's around. They've got to see me come out of here. Oh, well, let's hope the manager is taking his nap."

"Vic, you're getting me all mixed-up."

"I have to go. I'm sorry I mixed you up, but I'll bet you get yourself un-mixed by the time I get back. And then you know what we're going to do? We're going to take you out to see Las Vegas. We're going to have *fun*. When was the last time you had fun?"

"February 1949," I said sarcastically.

"Atta girl! Turn the TV on if you want but just the picture. You can take a shower, too. I sneaked some towels in, and a sheet. They're over there. But shower now if you're going to, before anyone checks into the room next door. See you later, alligator."

"In a while, crocodile," I replied automatically—but he was already out the door.

For a moment I just stood there, staring at the door. I guess I hoped Vic would suddenly come back in and explain the whole thing to me. I certainly couldn't understand it.

Here I had told him the most terrible thing about myself, the secret that I'd been keeping for almost a year. He should have been shocked, or horrified, or *something*. I was prepared for almost any reaction from Vic; I sure wasn't prepared for no reaction at all.

But the door didn't open and Vic didn't come back in. I shook my head helplessly. I was very sure I wasn't going to get myself un-mixed-up by four-thirty.

So I took a shower.

There was no soap in the bathroom, so all I could do was run the water as hot as I could stand it, and scrub myself with the hand towel Vic had brought. I didn't have any talcum powder, deodorant, or perfume, I realized, as I dried myself off. And I had to get back into the same crummy clothes I'd been wearing for days.

I turned the television on. I turned the volume up just the tiniest bit, enough so I could almost hear it when I sat two inches away from the screen. I was sure nobody in the next room would be able to hear it.

One of the channels was showing a Shirley Temple movie. Shirley was the daughter of a pilot and she practically lived on the air base. Her father was crazy about her. He was always picking her up and hugging and kissing and cuddling her. All the other pilots loved her too. She was the darling of the whole airport.

She didn't have a mother, as far as I could tell, but it didn't seem to bother her very much. Well, why should it? Her father loved her enough to make up for it, not to mention all the other pilots fussing over her.

I haven't seen many Shirley Temple movies, but I've seen enough to know that Shirley never had any trouble getting people to love her. She always had plenty of "what every child needs."

I turned the set off, disgusted with Shirley Temple. How come she never had any trouble finding people to love her? Even when she played an orphan, there were always twelve people around fighting over who'd get to adopt her. And why? Just because she was cute?

I'm pretty, and no one ever wanted to adopt me. The only thing being pretty had gotten me was trouble.

Oh, come on, I told myself. You can't be jealous of Shirley Temple.

Yes I can.

Every child needs love. Everybody loved Shirley Temple. Nobody loved me. Maybe it was silly, but was it really any wonder I was jealous of Shirley Temple? It might even have been better if I'd been a child star and just played parts like the ones Shirley played. Maybe that would have been almost as good as really being loved.

Well, I wasn't a child star. But when I did get to be a star—if I ever did—my fans would love me, and that would be even better.

Was that why Vic thought I *really* wanted to be an actress?

But what's wrong with wanting the public to love you? It's only natural.

Natural.

I remembered what Vic said about me and Uncle Ted. I didn't want to think about it, but there it was. How could those feelings be natural? They weren't natural, they were disgusting. Vic must have just said that to try and make me feel better.

Vic was so nice. The nicest person I ever met. And I felt so comfortable with him. I was able to talk with him, tell him everything, my deepest secrets, my inmost feelings, when I'd only known him a couple of hours.

And sitting on his lap, his arms around me, holding me close . . . even if I *was* crying my eyes out, those were the most wonderful few minutes of my whole life. I'd never felt so safe, so warm, so *loved*.

He loved me. I knew right then that Vic loved me. He loved me enough to risk his job for me, to spend his hard-earned money that he needed for medical school on a deluxe lunch for me, to hug me and kiss me but *not* to try anything else, even if we both wanted to.

It was wonderful! I closed my eyes and sighed. He was the person I'd been waiting for all my life. He would love me and take care of me and everything would be all right from now on.

I felt this tremendous surge of happiness swelling up inside me like a balloon. I didn't know how I could wait till four-thirty for Vic to come back. I wanted to tell him right now. I wanted to say, "I love you, too." I wanted to tell him I finally knew what love was.

If nobody had ever loved me before, well, I hadn't loved anyone either. In a way, I was almost glad. I had years and years of love saved up, and I wanted to give it all to Vic.

I turned the TV back on, just to make the time go faster. I think Shirley Temple's father had just been killed. She was crying and the other pilots were trying to comfort her.

I watched for a minute. Then I whispered, "Tough tarts, Shirley," and switched the channel.

When Vic came back I wanted to throw myself in his arms and yell, "I love you!" at the top of my lungs. But the minute he walked in the door I felt this big wave of shyness come over me. It was really strange. Even though a girl isn't supposed to tell a boy she loves him before he tells her, I thought it was different with us.

I mean, even though he hadn't actually told me right out he loved me, I was sure he did. "Actions speak louder than words," they always say, and Vic's actions proved how he felt about me.

But something held me back. Maybe it was the way I'd shocked him by kissing him so hard before. Maybe I was afraid he'd push me away again, like he had this morning. Even though I was sure he'd stopped me from kissing him so we wouldn't get carried away, I couldn't stand for that to happen now. And besides, a girl is certainly not supposed to kiss a boy first. That's probably why he was so surprised. Well, I wouldn't make that mistake again. I didn't want to do anything that would upset Vic.

So I just said, "Hi," very softly and turned off the TV.

"I'm sorry I had to run off like that. Everything okay?"

"Yes, fine. Especially now that you're here." I said that almost in a whisper, but I know he heard me.

He looked so cute. He was wearing a western shirt with a sort of tie made of string, and chino pants and a silver belt buckle. He was carrying a large paper bag.

"You look like a cowboy," I said. "And I have nothing to wear but this."

"No. You'll look like a beautiful senorita. See?" He reached into the bag and pulled out a white blouse and a bright, multicolored skirt that looked like it was made of yards and yards of tiny flowers. "At least, I hope you will. I thought they'd fit. They're my sister's."

The blouse was an off-the-shoulder peasant style which nobody in New York had worn for years. I wouldn't be able to wear it off the shoulders, because I didn't have a strapless bra, but that wouldn't be so bad. The trouble was that the skirt was really full, with a ruffle in the middle, and then even fuller below the ruffle.

"Did you bring any crinolines?" I asked, holding up the skirt to see how long it was.

"Crinolines?"

"Yeah, you know, to wear under the skirt. To make it stand out."

"Oh, petticoats. Gee, no, I never thought of that. I'm sorry."

"It doesn't matter. Really. It was so nice of you to go to all this trouble."

It did matter though. I wouldn't look like a beautiful senorita at all, I'd look positively frumpy with the skirt hanging off me all limp and saggy. And what if we went dancing? The skirt wouldn't even twirl out when I turned.

And I wanted to look beautiful for Vic. I wanted him to see me the way I looked when I left New York, all dressed up, with makeup and my Teena Paige dress, which I'd never see again. Maybe he was thinking that I was silly to imagine I could get into the movies, but if he saw me looking my best he'd know I wasn't kidding myself. And he'd want me to kiss him. And he'd want to kiss me back. And he'd forget I was only fifteen.

I went into the bathroom and put on the clothes. There was no full-length mirror in there, so I couldn't tell how I looked from the waist down, but I was pretty sure I didn't look like a beautiful senorita. The blouse fit okay, even though the elastic in the sleeves was a little loose, but the skirt was a size too big around the waist. And it did sag, halfway down my legs.

I hoped Vic wouldn't be ashamed to be seen with me. I

mean, even when peasant blouses were in style, they weren't supposed to make you look like a peasant.

"Sylvie?" he called. "Did you think about what I said?"

"Yes. Well, sort of. I mean, I did a lot of thinking and I'm not mixed-up anymore."

"Great."

I put on lipstick and sighed. There was nothing else I could do with what I had. I walked out of the bathroom slowly, almost wishing that Vic wasn't there to see me like this.

"Well," said Vic. He looked me over, like he was studying me. "Well."

I didn't know what to say. I looked down at the floor. I was sure he thought I looked awful, but I didn't want to seem ungrateful after all the trouble he'd gone to.

"Boy, I think you could put on a potato sack and look terrific," he said brightly.

I almost said I would *rather* be wearing a potato sack than this, because I couldn't look worse. But I didn't.

"Now, you're going to forget everything in the world except that you're a beautiful senorita out to have a good time." He blew on his fingernails and rubbed them against his chest. "With a handsome cowboy."

Well, at least he wasn't ashamed to be seen with me. And maybe he didn't think I looked as bad as I thought I did. After all, without a full-length mirror, I couldn't really tell.

"Okay." I forced out a smile. "Let's go."

Vic went out first and told me to follow him a minute later.

I walked as casually as possible past the pool, past the office, and met him on the street across from the Lucky

Silver Horseshoe Motel. I wondered where Walter was. I didn't see the Pontiac in the parking lot. Maybe he'd left Las Vegas and gone back to Fort Wayne. I hoped so.

Vic had borrowed his father's car for the evening.

"Now," he said, "we're off to fabled Fremont street, where you can lose more money in one night than you'll earn in your entire lifetime."

"I don't have any money to lose," I said.

"Then you'll be one of the few people to leave Las Vegas richer than when you came."

I thought that over for a moment. "That doesn't make any sense."

He opened the car door and looked down at me as I settled into the front seat. "Do you care?"

"No."

"Me neither."

He got into the car and we set out to see Las Vegas.

For the first couple of hours Vic took me around to see all the famous casinos. The Golden Nugget, Harold's Club, the Horseshoe Club. I realized I could have been dressed in my capri pants and nobody would have noticed, because the casinos were mobbed with people dressed in everything from cocktail dresses and evening gowns to toreador pants and Bermuda shorts. There were even little old ladies in housedresses and bedroom slippers playing slot machines wherever we went.

Some of them wore a glove—just one glove, on the hand they used to pull the slot machine lever. I asked Vic about that.

"So they won't get blisters on their hands."

"Blisters?"

"Yeah, after a couple of hours—"

"A couple of *hours? They* stand there like that for *hours?"*

"Sometimes all night."

I shook my head. I couldn't understand that at all.

But as the evening went on, the excitement and color and noise of the casinos began to get to me. I started to see why Walter liked Las Vegas. Even if you weren't gambling yourself, just watching the other people at the roulette wheel, the dice table, playing blackjack, was like being in a movie.

I mean, people actually were winning and losing thousands of dollars right in front of your eyes. It was positively *dramatic* to see people practically faint at the turn of a single card, or almost drool when the guy at the roulette table pushed this whole stack of chips toward him with a little rake-shaped stick.

And at the dice table, whole crowds would gather to groan or cheer as the game was played and somebody went on a winning streak or lost everything on one roll. Somehow, watching the people cheering and groaning for the players made me think of all the movies I'd seen about gladiator contests in ancient Rome.

But probably the most exciting thing I saw in the casinos was $1,000,000 in the Horseshoe Club. An actual $1,000,000 in $10,000 bills, framed in plate glass, shaped like a horseshoe. I just stood there, staring and staring at it—along with a lot of other people. Some of them were having their pictures taken in front of it. Vic could hardly drag me away.

"I've never seen a million dollars before," I kept saying.

"Neither has anybody else," Vic kept answering. "That's why it's here."

"Aren't they afraid someone will steal it?"

"This is probably the safest place in the world to display a million dollars. It's always crowded, it's never closed, how could anyone break the glass and run off without being caught?"

"I guess so. Isn't it beautiful?" I sighed.

Vic shrugged. "It's money. If you think money is beautiful . . ."

"You do if you don't have any."

Vic smiled. "Good point."

One of the reasons Vic was so anxious to get me away from that display in the Horseshoe Club was because we weren't even supposed to be there in the first place. You're not allowed to hang around the casinos if you're under twenty-one, so we didn't stay in any one spot for very long.

After we toured the casinos, Vic drove to the Strip, where all the big, famous hotels are. Vic took me to the dinner show at the Sands, and it was just like a nightclub. They had a lot of beautiful showgirls, and a whole stage show, including an act by Peter Lind Hayes and Mary Healy, which made me laugh so hard I almost choked on my dinner (which was very good, by the way). They were doing a sort of takeoff on gangster movies. I don't remember all of it, except that everybody was nicknamed after a color—like Blackie, Brownie, Whitey—and Peter Lind Hayes kept lighting cigarettes and sticking them in his mouth till he was smoking about seven cigarettes all at once.

After the show we went to another hotel, where they had dancing in the "Congo Room," and Vic and I danced to a live orchestra. Vic said he wasn't a very good dancer, and I said that was okay because I wasn't either; I didn't get very much practice.

Actually, he *wasn't* a very good dancer, but I didn't care. I loved him holding me during the slow dances. I thought he must be able to feel my heart beating against his chest, but that was okay because I wanted him to know I loved him.

It was strange, though, that he mostly wanted to dance cha chas and lindys, where you don't stay close to your partner but have to move around a lot and do tricky steps. Usually someone who doesn't dance very well would rather do the fox-trot than anything else. I figured he was doing the other dances because he thought I liked them better and he was just trying to be considerate.

My skirt hardly swirled out at all when I turned.

I didn't care.

Finally Vic said we ought to get back to the Lucky 7-11 Motel because we might have to scout around a little before we could sneak me into the empty room.

Vic had spent an awful lot of money on me, I knew, but when I started to say something about it in the car, he shushed me.

"Did you have fun?"

"The best time of my whole life," I sighed.

"Then I got my money's worth."

Vic drove to the drugstore near the motel so I could buy some magazines. As we were about to walk out, Vic pointed to a slot machine.

"Why don't you try it, Sylvie?" he whispered. The owner of the store was in the back, waiting on someone else. I hadn't played any of the machines in the casinos because you're not allowed to gamble if you're under twenty-one, and Vic said they watch you like a hawk there because the casinos are very law-abiding.

"Oh, no, I'm not a gambler." But my eyes must have lit up with excitement. I really did want to try it—just once. Only I didn't want to take any more money from Vic, and certainly not for gambling.

"Come on," he urged, "it's only a nickel machine. You can't leave Las Vegas without trying it *once.*" He handed me a nickel and I put it in and pulled the lever down.

The pictures in the little slots whirled and whirred and clicked into place and all of a sudden a pile of nickels came gushing out of the machine.

"Jackpot!" Vic yelled. I shrieked with excitement, and the salesclerk and two customers came rushing to the front of the store to see what had happened.

"I won!" Vic yelled, before I could say anything. "I hit the jackpot! Eight bucks!" Everyone smiled and said congratulations as Vic gathered up the money and started pouring it into my pocketbook. "Hold this for me, will you?" He winked at me.

I was so excited that I was jumping as we left the store, actually jumping up and down. "I won," I whispered, "I won, I won! Let's go play another one!"

"No," said Vic sternly. "You'll end up like one of those little old ladies with gloves."

"I will not."

"You will too. That was beginner's luck. You'll spend this whole eight bucks trying to win again. Just hold on to it."

"It's so *heavy*," I said happily. I lifted my pocketbook up and down.

"I'll change it into bills for you tomorrow. Come on. Let's get back to the motel."

We walked down the block to where Vic had parked his car. We were right across the street from the Lucky 7-11. We started to cross, when a car coming around the comer screeched to a stop only a couple of feet in front of us. Vic grabbed my arm to pull me back to the curb.

The car door flew open and a man came charging out.

"Sylvie! Where the hell have you been?"

Chapter 17

"Walter!"

I shrank back against Vic and he put his arm around me, like he was protecting me.

"I've been looking all over for you! Where have you been? Why did you walk out on me?" He turned to Vic. "Who are you?" He really glared at him, like he was going to challenge him to a duel or something.

"I'm a friend of Sylvie's," Vic said.

"You sure make friends fast, Sylvie." Walter's voice was real sarcastic. I knew he was thinking about Jim. He reached out like he was going to grab my arm. Vic pulled me back away from him and sort of pushed himself between me and Walter.

"What the hell is going on here?" Walter growled. "We were supposed to get married today, did she tell you that?"

"She told me a lot of things," Vic said. I didn't know how he could stay so calm. I was shaking like a leaf.

"Mr. Murchison, if you'd cool down a little, I think we all ought to go someplace and discuss this like civilized adults. There are a few things—"

"Civilized *adults?*" Walter was practically screaming, right there in the middle of the street. "I don't have anything to discuss with you, you little snot-nose. This is between me and Sylvie."

"Look, I don't blame you for being upset," Vic said. "After driving her all the way here from Indiana, crossing all those state lines ..."

"What are you talking about?" Walter's eyes narrowed. He looked at Vic suspiciously.

"Sylvie can't marry you. Not even in Las Vegas. Not even if she wanted to."

"She wants to. She told me she would. Didn't you, Sylvie? We had it all planned." Walter's voice was suddenly almost pleading. I felt terrible. I couldn't look at him.

"She's only fifteen."

I heard a sort of choked little gasp. I looked up, and saw, even under the pale light of the streetlamp, that Walter's face had turned almost white.

"She was in trouble, and you helped her out. But you crossed a lot of state lines bringing her here. . .

"I wanted to marry you," Walter said hoarsely. His face looked awful. "You told me you were eighteen."

"Walter, I'm sorry," I whispered. "I really am. I didn't know what else to do. I'll pay you back every penny you spent on me, I promise. I really mean that. I just—"

Walter kind of slumped against the lamppost, shaking his head.

"Walter?" My voice shook. "Walter, my things are still in your car. Could I have them? They're all I have left."

Walter stared at us, then, almost like a zombie, he walked in slow motion to the car and opened the trunk. He pulled out my hatbox, my pink dress, and my three crinolines, and handed them to me.

Walter stood there for a minute, staring at me, his mouth working as if he was trying to say something but couldn't get it out.

Finally he slammed the trunk closed and leaned on it heavily for a moment. "Good luck with your screen test, Sylvie. Not that you'll need it." He laughed, a short, bitter laugh. "You're a great little actress."

"Walter, I—" But Vic held my arm and shushed me. Walter got into his car. The motor turned on with a roar, and the Pontiac peeled out like a hot rod and disappeared down the street.

"Oh, *Vic.*" I thought I'd faint on the spot. "Oh, I feel terrible. That was awful. I feel like such a rat. He really *must* have loved me, Vic. I mean, he wanted to marry me and everything. . ."

"Come on, Sylvie. Let's get back to the room." Vic's voice was sharp, almost like he was angry with me.

We crossed the street to the Lucky 7-11 and sneaked into the vacant room without any trouble. Vic stopped me from turning on the light. Instead, he turned on the TV picture so there was just this dim glow from the set. It was sort of romantic.

I put my stuff on the bed and Vic sat down on the chair. He let out a deep whoosh of breath, and I realized that maybe he hadn't been as calm and cool as he seemed with Walter. That's why he had sounded so annoyed with me. He'd probably been as nervous as I was. But he'd protected me. Because he loved me.

I wanted to go and sit on his lap again, but I was afraid of being too forward. I was sure it was only a matter of time before he would make the first move.

"Vic, what was all that stuff about crossing state lines? I didn't know what you were talking about. Why did that get Walter so upset?"

"Because of the Mann Act." Vic's voice sounded kind of distant, like his mind was someplace else.

"What's the Mann Act?" I wanted him *not* to be distracted, not to be thinking of anything but me. We were here, together, alone. We loved each other. Why didn't he concentrate on *that?*

"Taking minors across state lines for immoral purposes. He must have broken the law about seven times getting you from Indiana to Nevada. That's why he flipped when he found out your real age. Probably why he gave up so easily too."

"Vic?"

"What?"

"Except for Walter, I had a wonderful time tonight. The best time in my whole life."

"I'm glad. You deserve it."

"Did you have a good time?"

"Yes."

I guess he was still shook up about the argument with Walter. Well, I was a little too, but with Vic here to love me and take care of me, I didn't want to keep thinking about Walter. Especially because I knew I would see his shocked, hurt face in my mind for a long, long time.

Vic just kept sitting there, brooding, until I couldn't stand it anymore. What does it matter who makes the first move? I asked myself. We love each other, that's all that counts. Maybe he's just shy. Maybe he doesn't want to rush me. Maybe he thinks I'm too young.

I walked over to the chair and sat down on the armrest. I put my hand gently on his cheek. He reached up and took hold of my wrist, pulling my hand to his lips. He kissed the back of it, then the palm. It was so romantic I thought I'd die.

"Oh, Vic," I breathed. I bent down and kissed him on the temple, on the cheek, on the bridge of his nose.

He made a funny little sound in his throat and pulled me onto his lap. He wrapped his arms around me and kissed me on the mouth. I kissed him back till I thought the room was spinning. Then he was kissing my neck, my shoulders, my ears, my eyelids, and I thought I would never catch my breath again. I wanted him to crush me against him, tight, tighter. I hugged him as hard as I could and pulled his head against my chest.

"I love you," I cried. "Oh, Vic, I love you so much."

He whispered something. I thought it was, "No, you don't," but I wasn't sure. He kept kissing me and stroking my back and my neck and we stayed that way for a long time—only it didn't seem like nearly long enough. Not when I could have stayed in his arms forever.

"Sylvie? You'd better get up now."

I put my head on his shoulder and tried to snuggle even closer against him. I didn't want him to stop kissing me. Ever.

"No, I mean it. Go sit on the other chair."

"Why? Don't you like kissing me?"

"Very much. That's why I want you to go and sit on the other chair."

"I guess I'm not very good at it," I said sadly. "I mean, I haven't any experience—"

"Then you're a natural. And if you don't get off me I'm going to stand up and dump you right on the floor."

I giggled. "You wouldn't."

He made a sort of strange little choking sound. I thought maybe he was getting angry, so I pulled myself off his lap. My knees felt weak as I went to sit on the edge of the bed. I didn't want to make Vic angry. Not when he made me feel like *this*.

It seemed like a long time before Vic looked up at me.

"Sylvie, you said you weren't mixed-up anymore."

"About some things. Some parts I couldn't figure out."

"Which parts?"

"The part about Uncle Ted—you know." I looked away from him, over at the TV screen. "Do we have to talk about this now? Everything was so nice, and you told me to forget about all my problems. . . ."

"I know. But if we don't talk now, we might end up making you more problems."

I figured he must have been worrying about getting carried away and losing control and getting me in trouble and that was why he wanted to talk instead of making out anymore. So I just sighed and turned to face him and said, "Okay. Let's talk, then."

"You never felt loved, did you?"

"Not until now," I said shyly.

Vic took a deep breath. "Listen. This is sort of complicated. You don't go out with boys much—"

"I don't go out with boys at all."

"But you have certain normal, healthy feelings that all girls your age have. You know what I mean?"

I looked down at my hands.

"Sylvie? You liked it when we were kissing?"

"You know I did," I whispered.

"Okay. Good. So you have these feelings, but what can

you do about them? Now, here's Uncle Ted acting affectionate toward you, and no one else in your whole life ever has. See what I'm getting at?"

"Not exactly. If I went out with boys I wouldn't feel this way about Uncle Ted?"

Even in the dim, flickering light from the TV screen, I could see Vic was frowning. "I'm not sure. Maybe. I told you this was complicated. I'm just trying to figure it out from what's in my psych books. But why I said it was natural was because you always wanted somebody to love you, and Uncle Ted's acting like he loves you—or at least, wants to make love to you. And one part of you says that's wrong, but another part of you wants it."

"But that's not love!" I cried. "That's sex."

"Sometimes people don't know the difference. Maybe you want to kid yourself into believing that if you let your foster father make love to you, that would be like having a father who loved you."

"You must think I'm a real jerk!"

"Yeah, sometimes I do."

"What?"

"Not about this, but—"

"About what?" I said coldly.

He jumped up and started pacing around the room. "Well, for crying out loud, Sylvie, *look* at yourself. You run away from home with a hundred and thirty bucks and have this fantasy that you're going to be a famous movie star before your hundred and thirty bucks runs out."

"That's not true! I never expected—"

"You get into a car with a guy you never saw before, he tries to attack you in a motel room, and what do you do?

You get right back in the car with him and let him drive you to Las Vegas. Am I supposed to think that's smart? Do *you* think that's smart?"

"He said he loved me," I whispered angrily.

"Didn't you tell me yourself you thought it might just have been sex?"

"Well, maybe at first," I admitted. "But then, after he got to know me—"

"He only knew you four days! How well could he get to know you in four days?"

"Well enough to want to marry me."

"So he could sleep with you. You know damn well that's why. You're not stupid. You've done some stupid things, but you're not stupid. And if a thirty-five-year-old man can mix up love and sex, is it so crazy that a fifteen-year-old girl might?"

For a while I didn't say anything. I was angry and confused. How could I get so mixed-up as to think that if I let Uncle Ted do what he wanted, it would be the same as having a loving father? A father doesn't do *that*.

Besides, I'd spent so many years thinking about my mother, I didn't even think that much about not having a father. As far as I knew, my father was dead. No one had ever mentioned him to me. Maybe he was killed before I was born or something. I never expected to find my father, like I expected someday to find my mother. So why would I look for a father in Uncle Ted?

It was complicated. It bothered me, what Vic said, but it also bothered me, maybe even more, that he thought I'd acted like a jerk. Maybe I hadn't acted like the smartest person in the world, but what other choices did I have?

I *had* to ran away.

From Uncle Ted. From my feelings.

From myself.

I'd never tried to explain what I felt about Uncle Ted, I just did. And every time I'd felt it, I'd tried to turn it off, make it go away, hide it even from myself. It was something I never wanted to think about, let alone sit down and try to figure out. All I knew was that it was wrong and bad.

And now Vic said it was natural.

I'd never been so confused in my whole life. But one thing I wasn't confused about. One thing I knew for sure.

"I know how I feel about you," I said softly. I didn't look at Vic, just looked down at the floor.

"How do you know? You just met me this morning."

"I just know," I said stubbornly. "And besides, it doesn't feel like I met you this morning. It feels like I've known you for years."

"But you haven't. Sylvie, you haven't known *anyone* for years. You think I'm being nice to you, and you like kissing me, so you think you love me. You'd think you loved *anybody* who was nice to you."

"That's not true! And you love me too. You *must*. Otherwise, why would you—"

"Why do you want to be an actress?" Vic asked suddenly.

"Because I think I'd be good at it"

"Why else? I mean, there are probably lots of things you'd be good at. Why did you pick that?"

"Well, you know, to be famous, maybe have my mother see me in the movies, make a lot of money—"

"And the fans?"

"I thought about that."

"A lot of people would love you. Wouldn't you like that?"

"Anybody would like that!" I snapped.

"But not everybody needs it so much," Vic said gently.

"You *don't* love me." Suddenly there was a cold, hollow feeling in my stomach. I was alone again. Nothing was going to be all right. I *had* been kidding myself.

"How could you do this to me?" I cried. "Why did you do all this, how could you let me think—"

"Oh, Sylvie, you don't love me either. That's just what I mean. You're ready to think you're in love the minute someone does something nice for you. Or you think *they* love *you*. You're going to get yourself in trouble that way."

"I nearly got in trouble with you, didn't I?" I said nastily.

"You know that's not true."

"How could you? How could you kiss me and—you're just like all the others!"

"Didn't you want me to?"

"What kind of a reason is that?" I cried. "You did me a *favor?*"

"I did myself a favor," Vic said. "I wanted to and I enjoyed it. And so did you. What better reason is there?"

"*Love.*"

"Sylvie, I've kissed other girls, but I didn't marry any of them. And you'll kiss other boys before you marry anybody. That's not necessarily love. But it's not necessarily wrong."

I lay down across the bed and buried my face in the pillow.

How could everything be so terrible again so fast? How could I fall in love and have my heart broken all in the space of a few hours? Because, no matter what Vic said, I was sure he was wrong about one thing. I *did* love him. I would *always* love him.

"Sylvie." He came over and sat on the bed. He put his hand on my back. I wanted to forget everything he'd been saying and pull him down to kiss me and hold me again. But I knew he wouldn't let me.

"I do like you, Sylvie. You're sweet and pretty and I think you're the bravest girl I've ever met. I'm very . . . attracted to you, and I felt you were attracted to me. I didn't do anything I shouldn't have, did I?"

I couldn't answer him.

"Did I?" he repeated. "Did I step one inch out of line?"

"No," I whispered finally.

"I wanted to. I would have liked to. But in a very special way, I do love you. Not the way you mean it, but believe me, I care about you. And I wouldn't do anything to hurt you. Everything I've done has been because I—I feel for you."

It wasn't enough. It was something, but it wasn't enough. I guess I had really been imagining marrying Vic, and having him take care of me forever. That's what I thought would happen. That's what naturally happens when two people love each other, isn't it? But he didn't love me "that way." He just "felt for me." He felt *sorry* for me, that's what he meant.

I was cold, and Vic hadn't even turned the air conditioner on.

"Sylvie, what are you going to do now?"

"I don't know," I said miserably. "I didn't think about it. All I thought about was you. I guess I thought you'd take care of me. I don't know why I thought that. I've always had to take care of myself. I just thought you loved me, so . . ."

He stroked my back. "I'd like to take care of you, Sylvie. But I can't. I have eight more years of school before I become a doctor, let alone a psychiatrist, and you have a problem you can't wait eight years to solve. You know I'll help you as much as I can. But, help you do what? That's what we have to figure out. Do you still think you can go to Hollywood and try to get in the movies?"

I turned over on my back and stared up at the ceiling. I thought of Ruby Durban, my stolen wallet, Walter in the Blue Grass Motel, Walter screaming at me under the streetlight.

"No," I said. "Not yet."

"There's no reason why you can't try later, when you're eighteen, say."

"That's three years."

"I know. When you finish high school."

"You don't need to finish high school to get in the movies."

"But until you get your first break, you'll need a job. It would be easier to get a good job if you had a diploma."

"You don't need a diploma to be a model, either. That's what I was going to do till I got my first part."

"But what choice do you have? Even if you tried to stay here, eventually they'd find you and make you come back. You're a minor. You know they're looking for you. It's only a matter of time."

"I could stay with you. At your house. You could tell your parents I'm a friend from school or something."

"Sylvie, my father's a cop. Why do you think I didn't take you there in the first place instead of hiding you here? He's probably got your picture on the wire right now."

A cold shiver went down my spine. "Why didn't you tell me your father was a cop?"

"I didn't want you to worry that I'd turn you in. I was afraid you'd run away if you knew."

"But, Vic, all you did, hiding me and—doesn't that make you an accessory or something? Isn't that a crime?"

"Maybe technically. I don't know. I don't care. It would have been a crime *not* to do it. Anyway, that doesn't matter now. What are you going to do?"

"Maybe I could go to California, and when you go back to UCLA in the fall—"

"Sylvie, be realistic. That's the first place they'd look for you."

"No, no they wouldn't. They were looking in Rochester. That's where I told them I was going." I remembered the note I had left Aunt Grace, how clever I thought my plan was.

"That was five days ago. By now, every police department in the country has your description. And everyone knows you wanted to be in the movies. Don't you think they'll figure it out?"

Suddenly, clear as if it was happening right now, I saw myself writing the last letter to my mother from New York. I remembered how I told her my plan, and how Uncle Ted had come into the room while I was writing. Just like I was watching a movie, I saw myself grabbing the letter, crumpling it up, and sticking it in my bathrobe pocket. And then I saw myself taking off the bathrobe and kicking it under the bed. . . .

Vic was right. It was hopeless. For all I knew, every movie studio in Hollywood had been warned to be on the lookout for me. Every guard at every entrance gate might have a picture of me. The minute I set foot on a studio lot, they would be on the phone to the police.

"You mean I have to go back to New York?"

"I don't know what else you can do."

"Back to Aunt Grace and Uncle Ted?" I asked dully.

"Well, that's another question. Do you want to go back there?"

"Aunt Grace is okay. And Honey and Bunny. But. . ."

"Yeah, *but*. You have to decide whether you want to spend that much time running and hiding and locking doors."

"Or not running." My voice was barely a whisper, but Vic heard me.

"Oh, you'll run, honey. I trust you. You just have to trust yourself a little more. But—it's a hell of a way to live, isn't it?"

"How do I know the next place will be any better? It could be worse. There might be other things. I mean, except for Uncle Ted, everything was okay."

"I know. You're right, there's no way to tell whether the next place would be better. I guess you have to decide whether to stay with the problem you know, or to take a chance on the next place."

"Even if the social worker did believe me—"

"She'll believe you all right. I typed up a statement of all the things you told me about Uncle Ted and got it notarized."

"What does that mean?"

"It means that I swear in front of a notary public that everything in that paper is true. And it has my phone number and address in it. I'm your witness. If they don't believe you, you can show them that statement. They can call me long distance or I could even come to New York and testify, if they want. But I don't think they'd want to make such a big stink about this."

"I hope you have to come to New York," I said. "I can't stand it that I'm never going to see you again."

"Why do you say that? Who says you're never going to see me again? There are buses, trains, planes. I have vacations. And I'll write to you, if you promise to write to me every week and tell me you're okay. Or if you're *not* okay."

"You'll come and see me? Will you write to me every week too?"

"Every week as long as you want me to. And I'll come and see you. Do you think when you go back to New York tomorrow I'm going to forget I ever met you? I'll *never* forget you, Sylvie. I'll always be here if you need me. All you have to do is write, or phone, or *yell.*"

"Oh, Vic, I don't care if you believe it or not, I love you."

He pushed my stuff off the bed and lay down next to me. He slid his arm under my shoulder.

I won't cry, I promised myself. As long as he's here with me, I won't cry. Even if I do have to go back, at least I'll have somebody real to write to now. Somebody who'll wait for my letters and answer them, and help me if I need help. And in three years ...

"Vic?" I whispered.

"What?"

"When you're a doctor, I'll be twenty-three. I wouldn't be too young then."

"You might even be famous by then." I couldn't see his

face, but I could hear the smile in his voice.

"But you won't get married until you're a doctor, will you?"

"No. How would I support a wife for eight years?"

"Then when I'm twenty-three, you'll still be single."

"I expect to be."

"Well then, maybe—"

He squeezed my shoulder. "Sylvie, we don't know what's going to happen the day after tomorrow. Let's not think about eight years from tomorrow."

"All right," I said. But I *would* think about it. I wanted to. I didn't want to think about the day after tomorrow.

I snuggled against him and he put his arms around me and held me close and his chest was my pillow and he stayed with me all night long.

And in the morning we made a long distance call to the Child Welfare Department in New York.

Acknowledgments

Special thanks to Celeste Watman for being so outrageously generous with her time and expertise; to Harvey Miller, for providing access to the legendary Miller Music Archives; to Sue Kostiuk, for her valiant battle with the Bureaucracy; and to my friends at the Massapequa Public Library, particularly Harry Weber.